So his favorite jewelry designer was single now.

He couldn't quite figure out how he felt about that. As time went on, his relationships were becoming shorter and shorter. In each of the past three, Tony had become restless after mere months.

And each ending brought him back to Rachel.

What was it about Rachel Palmer that captivated him so? Part of it, he supposed, was that she remained a puzzle. They'd known one another for five years, ever since he'd walked into her quaint little shop on a whim and had admired a necklace one of the clerks was wearing.

"This is Mrs. Palmer's design."

Mrs. Palmer. Tony had never been able to figure her out.

She was very different from the other women he knew, personally and professionally. She was all business all the time. She never let her hair down, figuratively or otherwise. Today, however, he'd glimpsed a softer side, just a hint of vulnerability that left him intrigued.

And there was the not so small matter that she was no longer a Mrs.

Dear Reader,

Every woman knows a Tony Salerno, whether or not he comes with a sexy Italian accent. Charming, handsome men with a bedroom smile who like to flirt and can make a woman feel ridiculously feminine with a simple glance or smile. But do such men make good husbands?

Rachel Palmer is sure they don't, which was why she married a man like Mal. Staid, predictable, boring Mal, who winds up having an affair with his secretary. So much for Rachel's theory. So much for playing it safe.

Now she's left to ponder a question: If she was so far off the mark with Mal, might she also be dead wrong about Tony?

I hope you enjoy *If the Ring Fits....* As always, I like to hear what you think. Email me through my website at www.jackiebraun.com or become a fan of Romance Author Jackie Braun on Facebook.

Best,

Jackie Braun

JACKIE BRAUN

If the Ring Fits...

HARLEQUIN®

entertain, enrich, inspire™

Recycling programs
for this product may
not exist in your area.

ISBN-13: 978-0-373-17834-6

IF THE RING FITS...

First North American Publication 2012

www.Harlequin.com

Printed in U.S.A.

Jackie Braun is a three-time RITA® Award finalist, a four-time National Readers' Choice Awards finalist and the winner of a Rising Star Award for traditional romance fiction. She can be reached through her website, www.jackiebraun.com.

"There is something about an Italian accent that just screams romance. But ultimately actions speak louder than words."
—Jackie Braun

Books by Jackie Braun

THE PRETEND PROPOSAL
THE PRINCESS NEXT DOOR
MR. RIGHT THERE ALL ALONG
THE DADDY DIARIES
INCONVENIENTLY WED!
A DINNER, A DATE, A DESERT SHEIKH
CONFIDENTIAL: EXPECTING!
BOARDROOM BABY SURPRISE

Other titles by this author available in ebook format.

For Andrea Cerofolini and Meredith Fridline.
Grazie!

CHAPTER ONE

"I'M divorced." Rachel Palmer raised her chin after saying so and affected a smile.

Hmm. She sounded defensive. She wrinkled her nose at her reflection in the mirror and tried again.

"I'm no longer married." This time she added a careless shrug to the mix. It didn't help.

Hands on her hips, she announced baldly, "That's right. Mal has been doing the nasty with his secretary, and I was the last to know."

Sucker.

Maybe she should just stamp that on her forehead and be done with it. If only it were that simple.

As Rachel was discovering, divorce wasn't an ending. Nor was it a beginning exactly. It was a transition. An emotional, a physical and, certainly, a financial shift of seismic proportions. The problem was she had no idea where she would wind up once the tectonic plates of her life settled down again.

She needed to figure it out and fast. As of yesterday afternoon, her marriage was officially over, decreed so not only by the two parties involved but by the state of Michigan. Rachel Palmer, née Preston, was a single woman once more. She wrinkled her nose again at her reflection. A single woman inching toward thirty-three and past her prime child-bearing years, as her mother so help-fully had pointed out during dinner the previous evening.

Dinner had been Heidi's idea. Her younger sister said they should go to Maxie's, the same upscale restaurant where Mal had proposed, and celebrate.

"It will be like erasing the past. A do-over. Come on, Rach. Now isn't the time for mourning," Heidi had insisted cheerfully as they'd left the Oakland County courthouse.

Against her better judgment, Rachel had agreed. She'd regretted it as soon as a round of fruit-garnished drinks arrived at their table. While their mother nibbled pineapple off the skewer, Heidi had raised her glass.

"Here's to the start of an exciting new chapter in your life."

Exciting new chapter? Her sister should have been named Pollyanna. It fit her perpetually optimistic personality.

Rachel had reached for her water. "Heidi—"

"If you're free tomorrow night, I have someone interested in meeting you. We can double date."

"Heidi—" Once again that was as far as she'd got before her sister cut her off.

"Oh, don't worry. He's nice and harmless." The younger woman had scrunched up her face and taken another sip of her overly sweet drink. "Kind of boring, actually, but he's polite and well-groomed. The first guy doesn't count anyway. Everyone understands he'll just be your rebound man."

"I don't think this week will work for me." Or the next, or the next...indefinitely. But Rachel knew her sister. It was best to leave it open and save herself the inevitable argument.

"You haven't been out in ages, Rach."

Rachel's mouth had fallen open at that. "I just got divorced. Today."

Their mother had made an indelicate snorting noise. "That didn't stop Mal."

Heidi had taken a more diplomatic approach. "You and Mal were legally separated for the past year. You even stopped wearing your wedding band three months ago."

"In part to get you off my back. You kept hounding me about it," Rachel had shot back.

Besides, the ring represented a promise, one that had been broken. But Rachel didn't agree with Heidi's assessment that she needed to get back into the dating scene right away. It wasn't that she still loved Mal. Oh, she mourned the demise of their marriage and the failure it represented, but she wasn't pining over her ex any longer. Even so, that didn't make the thought of dating again any more palatable.

Rachel's hollow-eyed self gazed back at her in the mirror now. She wasn't like her outgoing younger sibling, who could strike up a conversation with a stranger in the grocery store and then be invited out for dinner or drinks. She'd found meeting men awkward and intimidating when she was twenty-two. She didn't delude herself that it would be any easier as a divorced woman of thirty-two.

She turned on the faucet and splashed cold water on her face in the hope of obliterating the dark circles under her eyes. Unfortunately, they were still there after she blotted her face dry with the towel. She did her best to camouflage them with some concealer, and then added mascara to her lashes. They were long and thick and by far one of her best features. Maybe no one would notice the circles if she played up her lashes. After applying tinted moisturizer and a little blusher to her cheeks, she pulled her hair back in a clip. She might not be able to wrap her mind around

Heidi's "new chapter" description, but it *was* a new day. And it was time to get ready for work.

It was just before eight o'clock when she pulled her car into the nearly empty municipal lot behind Expressive Gems, the jewelry store she owned in Rochester's charming downtown. Not only did she sell jewelry, five years ago she'd begun to do some serious designing. When inspiration struck, she could lose herself in her job for hours. She'd entertained dreams that went beyond the little shop, dreams that hadn't seemed realistic or practical while married to Mal. Indeed, he'd discouraged them. He was unhappy as it was that so much of her time was taken up at the shop. But now? New day, new chapter. It was something to think about, she decided as she pulled the lapels of her coat together and hustled across the parking lot.

The weather was turning right along with the leaves. The wind didn't help. Another week and the trees that dotted the street out front would be aflame in hues of red and orange. Rachel liked autumn, although she couldn't help dreading the long Michigan winter that would come after it.

She let herself in via the employee entrance, balancing her purse and travel mug of coffee as she unlocked the door and deactivated the alarm. Then she switched off the interior security lights and flipped on the overheads. The aroma of roses hit her almost immediately. She kept a lush arrangement near the display cases in the front. They had another day, maybe two, before they would need to be replaced. Some had started to wilt.

Jewelry shopping was about mood and emotions. In particular, it was about romance. She suppressed the twinge of betrayal she felt thinking about the receipts for a high-end jewelry store across town in Mal's coat pocket that had led to the discovery of his infidelity. It was bad enough he'd cheated on her, but then he had to go and buy his bimbo jewelry at the store of a competitor who surely recognized his name.

A brisk knock sounded at the front entrance as she finished making a pot of coffee in the shop's small break room. The sign on the door clearly read Closed. She hadn't turned it over yet, nor would she for another forty-five minutes. As tempted as she was to ignore the interruption, she went to see who it was.

She had a licensed general contractor coming, though the appointment wasn't until ten o'clock. Perhaps he was early. Very early, she thought, glancing at the clock. Depending on where the estimate came in, Rachel was hoping to renovate the storage space over the shop and turn it into an apartment. The house she and Mal owned jointly was on the market. Per their settlement, the equity was to be split evenly between them when it sold. She planned to use her half to buy Mal's investment in Expressive Gems from him. The deed to the shop was in her name, but Mal was a cosigner on the loan she'd taken out to purchase inventory when she'd first started designing her own jewelry. That also was the deal they'd worked out through their lawyers.

While the housing market was slow, Rachel needed to get serious about finding a new place to live—hence the appointment with the contractor. When she'd first purchased the old building, she'd considered turning it into an income property. It had the potential to become a decent studio apartment. Then she and Mal had married and she'd put those plans on hold. Much like her career plans beyond the shop, she thought with chagrin.

When she reached the door, it wasn't the contractor who stood on the other side of the glass. It was Tony Salerno. The collar of his trench coat was flipped up against the damp breeze. His grin flashed white in his tanned face when he spotted her. The smile she offered in return was as polite as it was automatic. He was Expressive Gems's best customer, and as such, one of the few people for whom she would open early.

His smile said he knew it.

"Mr. Salerno. Good morning."

"Buongiorno, carina."

Despite her best efforts, gooseflesh pricked on her arms. In addition to being her best customer, Tony was hands down her most handsome, with hair the color of espresso and a pair of eyes that leaned toward hazel. His mouth was wide, sensual. When he conversed with members of the opposite sex, it curved into the sort of smile best saved for the bedroom. Add in the sexy remains of an Italian accent—he'd immigrated to the United States from Florence with his mother when he was thirteen—and he was never without female companionship.

Since Tony could afford to be generous, he never was without the need for glittery trinkets to bestow on those women. Hence his unofficial status as Expressive Gems's benefactor. Thanks to his regular patronage and appreciation for her work, she'd had the resources to devote to her own designs. Still, Rachel never felt completely at ease around him. He made her feel ridiculously feminine and self-conscious. That was especially true on this day, with her sister's talk of dating echoing in her head.

As he stepped inside, Rachel tucked behind her ears the mousy hair that had fallen out of her clip, and tried not to think about how long it had been since she'd gone in for highlights.

"This is a surprise," she said.

"A pleasant one, I hope." Before she could respond, he was chiding, "How many times must I ask you to call me Tony?"

He'd done so on half a dozen occasions already, but Rachel preferred the professionalism a courtesy title lent their relationship, as well as the distance it created. Flirting came as naturally to the man as breathing. She had four employees, all of them women, and all of them completely smitten. Rachel wasn't smitten. Married women didn't get smitten. She frowned as the realization dawned anew. She wasn't married any longer. Which meant it was perfectly acceptable to find Tony attractive and to flirt right back... if she wanted to.

"You are frowning," he remarked.

"I'm trying to recall the last time you visited Expressive Gems," she evaded. "It's been months."

"At least nine. Much, much too long." His gaze skimmed down from her face and he murmured, *"Che bella."*

Rachel exhaled softly between her teeth. If someone were to bottle up that sexy accent and sell it as an aphrodisiac, they could make a fortune. And that was before his voice dropped to a husky whisper and he asked, "Have you missed me?"

The gooseflesh was back. Or more likely it never had left.

"Of course, I have. After all, you're one of our favorite customers."

Not to mention the one whose patronage was going to help fund a good portion of the upstairs renovation.

He chuckled at her diplomatic dodge. "Your husband is a lucky man, *carina.*"

He'd made that very comment several times in the past. Should she correct him? She kept her smile in place and instead decided to let it pass. She folded her hands in front of her. Tony studied her, one side of his mouth turned up in consideration. While he appeared perfectly at ease, she discreetly nibbled the inside of her cheek. The coffee wasn't ready yet. In the quiet shop, she could hear the machine still gurgling away in the break room. She would offer him a cup when it finished. For now she said, "Let me take your coat."

"*Grazie.*"

As he slipped off the trench, she was determined not to let the conversation lapse again. "You're out and about early today."

"Jet lag. I just returned to town yesterday. I could not sleep. I have been up for hours." His smile turned apologetic. "I saw the lights on while I was on my way to the bakery for bagels and decided to take the chance that you would be willing to let me in a little early. *Allora*..." He shrugged.

He used that word a lot. She wasn't sure exactly what it meant, but it seemed to act as the Italian equivalent of "so."

"I got in early myself. I like to arrive before my employees. I get the coffee going and just relax for a little while."

"Ah, then I really must thank you for taking pity on me."

A man such as Tony Salerno inspired many emotions. Pity, however, was not among them.

As Rachel hung his trench on the coat tree next to the door, she caught a whiff of his cologne. The scent was sensual, sexy, sigh-worthy. The conversation she'd had the evening before with Heidi popped into her head.

The first guy doesn't count anyway. Everyone understands he'll just be your rebound man.

Tony Salerno would make one heck of a rebound.

What was she thinking?

Rachel tossed Tony's coat onto a hook and turned back to him with a guilty smile. Her tone was a little breathless when she said, "I'm afraid I have no bagels to offer, but the coffee is almost ready. Would you like a cup?"

"*Si, per favora.* I take it—"

"Black," she interjected.

His lips curved. "You remember."

It was her job to remember the preferences of her best customers. The fact that she couldn't think how any of her other regulars took their coffee didn't mean anything. She went to pour them each a cup.

When she returned to the showroom, he was sitting on a tall metal stool in front of the long glass case that held her designs. The heel of one supple leather loafer was hooked on the bottom rung. Despite his claim of jet lag, his appearance was impeccable. No bloodshot eyes. No dark circles. And his hair looked gently tousled rather than ravished by the wind. With his lean build, he wore clothes well, whether the style was casual or formal and sophisticated. Today he had on a toffee-colored sweater—she'd bet it was cashmere—and black gabardine trousers that probably cost more than the shop's monthly mortgage. He straightened when he saw her, and then stood to take one of the white porcelain mugs adorned with the shop's logo.

"Thank you, *signora.*"

Rachel's understanding of Italian was limited, but she understood courtesy titles. This made twice he'd referenced her marital state. She decided to correct him this time.

"Actually, it's miss now. I'm divorced." The words came out with surprising ease. Apparently, all of that practice in front of the bathroom mirror earlier had paid off.

"Signorina."

Tony said it slowly, almost as if testing the word on his tongue. Then his mouth curved with another of those toe-curling smiles that made her feel so self-conscious. She held the mug of steaming coffee close to her face and sipped, pretending to be unaware of the way he was studying her.

"Should I offer my condolences on the demise of your marriage?" he asked after a moment.

"Condolences? No," she said honestly. She set the coffee down on counter. In the case beneath it, the gemstones she'd worked into various designs winked as they caught the light. The sight always reminded her of Christmas. The holiday would be here before she knew it. It wouldn't be her first without Mal. They'd spent it apart last year, as well. She'd been sad then, shell-shocked by all of his deceptions. She was nobody's fool now.

Next to her, Tony sipped his coffee. "But I gather that congratulations would not be appropriate, either."

She nodded, surprised he understood, even more surprised when she confided, "My sister claims I'm starting an exciting new chapter in my life."

"This sister, is she older?"

"Younger. Just out of college."

"Well, younger or not, she is correct. Am I correct in thinking you do not quite agree?"

Rachel focused on the colorful gems. "It's all so new."

"If there is anything I can do…" Tony left it at that.

Several other people—Rachel's friends, her employees, Heidi and her mother—had made similar offers over the months as Rachel's attempts to resuscitate her marriage failed and she was forced to accept the inevitable. Tony's was probably rooted in politeness more so than practicality. They had no real relationship, after all, save for a business one. Even so, she appreciated the gesture.

"Thank you. That's kind."

His voice lowered and his gaze turned intense. "I say what I mean, *signorina*. If you need anything—anything— you have only to ask."

He laid a hand over hers as he said it. His fingers were long and tapered, and adorned with one simple gold ring that bore a crest of some sort. The design wasn't hers, but she admired the excellent workmanship. She focused on the ring, afraid to meet his gaze. She wasn't sure which had her more discombobulated, the heat radiating from his hand or the fact that he clearly meant what he said. Either way, she was being foolish. She had to swallow twice before she could speak and change the subject.

"So, where did your travels take you this time?" As surreptitiously as possible, she pulled her hand free and picked up her coffee mug once again.

Tony wrote features for a travel magazine that catered to upscale tastes. In fact, he owned the magazine, as well as a couple of others, all of which were based in New York and aimed at people who had more money than they could spend in five lifetimes.

He knew his target audience well, since he counted himself among their elite number. From the chatter of her employees, Rachel knew that in addition to an estate in well-heeled Rochester Hills, which he considered home since it was close to where his family lived, Tony kept an apartment in Manhattan, another in Rome and had executive suites on reserve at luxury hotels in both Paris and London.

He didn't need to work, but he'd once told Rachel that he enjoyed writing too much to sit back and let others have all the fun doing it for him. Rachel respected him for that, even if she didn't exactly respect his playboy lifestyle. The man went through women the way some people went through napkins. Still, no one could argue he wasn't generous with them, a fact she knew well since it benefited Expressive Gems's bottom line.

"I spent most of my time in Milan with trips to London, Paris, Monaco, Berlin and Stockholm."

"Is that all?" she drawled.

His shoulders rose at the same time the corners of his mouth turned down. The gesture was decidedly European. "I was working."

"You found some time to play, I trust."

His smile was quick and lethal. "I always find time to play. I would be a dull, dull boy otherwise. No?"

Dull and boy were two words Rachel would never think to use to describe the man before her. She cleared her throat. "So, what are you writing about now?"

"The best places to stay and dine during fashion week in each city, with a side piece on up-and-coming designers to watch."

"I suppose you had to interview a lot of models for that."

His careless shrug was at odds with his Casanova smile. "They have a unique perspective to offer."

"One model in particular, I'm guessing."

Again, the smile. "Astrid."

Rachel pictured a long-limbed and graceful beauty. "And you are here today looking for something special to give her. A token of your affection and appreciation?"

"Pazzesco!" He flashed a smile. "You know me too well."

Actually, what Rachel knew was his type. Tony was a lot like her absentee father, who'd left her mother when Heidi was barely out of diapers. Griff Preston had popped in and out of his daughters' lives since then, showering them with gifts that were a poor substitute for his time and affection.

"So, what are you thinking? A necklace? Perhaps a bracelet? Or maybe a pair of earrings?"

Tony never purchased a ring. Too much could be read in to that, he'd told her once, and she thought he had a point.

"A necklace, I think. Astrid has a lovely neck. It will make an exquisite showcase for one of your designs."

Rachel pulled out a pad of paper to jot down some notes. Already, ideas were flashing in her mind. She loved this part of the process.

"Let's talk about style. If you want to showcase her neck, perhaps a choker would be best. Something delicate, feminine. Maybe pearls, three or four rows, threaded together with silver wire."

But he was shaking his head. "A choker sits too high." He touched Rachel's neck. "I want something longer that falls about here." The tip of his finger glided slowly from the hollow of her throat to the lowest point visible in the V of her blouse. Her breath hitched.

"Ah. More of a pendant, then," she managed.

"Yes. Something to draw attention to her other assets."

"Why don't you tell me a little bit about Astrid?" It was standard practice. It helped Rachel with the design process. But she also couldn't help but be curious about the glamorous women Tony dated.

He rubbed his jaw. Even though he hadn't shaved, the dark stubble that shaded his jaw didn't do anything to detract from his appearance. "She's very interested in astrology and numerology, tarot cards."

"And her sign?" She said it tongue-in-cheek, but he answered with a straight face.

"Pisces."

"What does she look like, other than being gorgeous, since that much is a given?"

"Well, she is Swedish. Pale, creamy skin."

"Blonde?"

"Yes, with eyes nearly as blue as yours. Her lashes are not as lush, though."

He'd noticed her eyes? Rachel made a little humming noise in the back of her throat before asking, "And how old is she?"

"Twenty-three."

Ah. That made Astrid just a year younger than Mal's secretary.

"She's been modeling professionally since she was fourteen," Tony was saying.

"Fourteen, hmm. Where are those child-labor laws when you need them?"

"You think she is too young for me." His expression held more amusement than insult.

"I make no judgments," she said hastily. Then she exhaled and shook her head. "At least I shouldn't. I mean, who am I to judge anyone's relationship?"

"I am sorry, *carina*."

Embarrassed by her outburst as much as by the sympathy she saw in his eyes, Rachel got back to business.

"Does Astrid have a favorite gemstone?"

"Diamonds." His laughter rumbled and he shook his head. "I think a warmer stone would suit her better."

Tony never went for diamonds. He didn't have to tell Rachel that, as with the purchase of a ring, too much could be read into that particular stone, as well.

Rachel took the key ring from the pocket of her blazer, unlocked the case and retrieved a black-velvet-lined tray from the bottom shelf. Loose stones of various cuts, sizes and colors glittered under the lights.

"Do you see anything here that catches your eye? Don't worry about the cut or size. Anything you select I can cut and size to suit. We're just picking out a gemstone right now."

Tony settled on an aquamarine—Astrid's birthstone—in a triangular-shaped or "trilliant" cut that would be set in platinum. He wanted no less than three carats for the stone. As for the rest of the design, including the kind of chain, he left that to Rachel. She was thinking of something that would pull in Astrid's interest in astrology. She appreciated his trust in her artistic judgment. Some customers were so specific about what they wanted and they insisted on being so involved in the process that they left little room for creativity. In those cases, she was left to craft their vision. She much preferred conjuring up one of her own.

"When would you like to pick it up?" she asked as she wrote up the order.

"I will be in town for the next several weeks. Astrid will be in New York the last weekend in November for a magazine photo shoot. Would that be enough time?"

She did some quick calculations in her head. If the stone he wanted came in quickly from her supplier, it would be more than enough time. She had little else on her plate, professionally or personally.

"It shouldn't be a problem. Shall we say the Wednesday before Thanksgiving, then?"

Tony nodded as he rose. "Perfect. I cannot wait to see what you create."

The smile she gave him was fueled by genuine pleasure rather than mere politeness. Not only had designing jewelry paid her bills, during the past several months, it had saved her sanity.

She meant it when she said, "I'm very eager to get started."

"Until I see you again, *bella*."

"Yes. Until then."

CHAPTER TWO

THE weather outside was every bit as bitter as it had been before Tony had ducked into Expressive Gems. He turned up the trench's collar once again and tucked his hands into its lined pockets. As he made his way to the bakery, walking headlong into the wind, he started to whistle.

So, his favorite jewelry designer was single now.

He couldn't quite figure out how he felt about that. Nor could he explain why he hadn't mentioned to Rachel that the necklace he was having her make for Astrid was intended as a parting gift. He had ended things with the young model before returning to the States. The relationship had run its course.

Astrid was lovely, funny and far smarter than most people gave her credit for being, but they didn't have much in common except time to kill between fashion events in various European cities. And even there they'd differed. Where Tony gravitated to the classics in art, music and clothing, Astrid followed the trends. She wanted to stay out late and kick up her heels in the exclusive nightclubs, whereas Tony had tired of life in that fast lane years ago. Did that make him too old? Or Astrid too young, he mused? Regardless, he had grown bored quickly.

Indeed, as time went on, his relationships were becoming shorter and shorter. In each of the last three, Tony had become restless after mere months.

And each ending brought him back to Rachel.

He stopped whistling as he waited for the light to change so he could cross the street. What was it about Rachel Palmer that captivated him so? Part of it, he supposed, was that she remained a puzzle. They'd known one another for five years, ever since he'd walked into her quaint little shop on a whim and had admired a necklace one of the clerks was wearing.

"This is Mrs. Palmer's design."

Mrs. Palmer. Tony had never been able to figure her out.

She was very different from the other women he knew, personally and professionally. For starters, she was all business all of the time. She never let her hair down, figuratively or otherwise. In truth, Tony had always felt a little intimidated by her. Today, however, he'd glimpsed a softer side, just a hint of vulnerability that left him intrigued. And there was the not-so-small matter that she was no longer a Mrs.

His stomach growled loudly enough to be heard over the howl of the wind. Glancing up, he realized the light had changed back to red while he'd stood there ruminating over Rachel. *Pazzesco!* Crazy. After a shake of his head, Tony didn't bother waiting for the Walk sign to appear a second time. He crossed against the light, keeping an eye on the cars. There weren't that many. It was nearly nine o'clock and the traffic along Main Street was sparse. School was in session and most commuters were at work, starting their day. Meanwhile, he was on vacation.

Between writing a dozen features and putting out fires at the various publications under his control, he had earned a break, a long one, although he would make do with a week of being incommunicado before he checked in via phone at his New York offices. He preferred Rochester Hills to the hustle and bustle of the Big Apple. His mother and stepfather lived close by, as did his sister, Ava, her husband, Bill, and their two adorable daughters. He might not be interested in getting married and settling down, but he enjoyed being surrounded by family. When he was away for too long, he even missed his mother's good-natured nagging.

Besides, he didn't need to spend all of his time in Manhattan. The internet made it easy to stay in touch with the staff of his three magazines. Of course, the internet wasn't just changing his job, it was changing the way the publishing world operated.

The advent of the digital age and widespread access to the internet meant more and more of the people who subscribed to his magazines wanted the convenience of downloading content to the electronic device of their choosing. But others still preferred to receive magazines in the mail each month or pick them up at the newsstand, flipping through the glossy pages at their leisure.

Advertisers, meanwhile, simply wanted to reach their targeted demographic in the most cost-effective way possible. Tony's job was to keep them all happy while ensuring that the quality of his product never suffered.

Some people, most people, thought he had nothing to lose. Despite his success, they viewed his career as a mere hobby, a rich man dabbling in the publishing world to fill his time and stave off boredom. It was true that the magazines could fold and the greatest casualty for him personally would be his pride. He would get along fine on the trust fund left to him by his late father. But several hundred people worked for him in various capacities in various cities around the globe. They relied on the incomes they earned to raise their children and keep roofs over their heads. So while he believed in enjoying life and indulging his whims, he took his responsibilities as the head of the Fortuna Publishing Group very seriously.

His cell phone trilled just as he reached the bakery. Despite the inclement weather, he opted to take the call outside rather than disturb the customers who were enjoying coffee and pastries at a smattering of tables inside.

"Pronto."

"You are home?" It was his mother. There was no mistaking Lucia's voice or the worry in her tone.

"I am. I arrived late last night. I did not want to wake you," he added, knowing she would chide him for not calling.

She did. Then, "You will come for dinner tonight?" It was as much a command as a question. "Ava and her family will be here. I will make your favorite."

After months of restaurant fare, his mouth watered at the offer of a home-cooked meal. "Anything you cook is my favorite, Mama."

"So my job is easy. Come early." He heard her laugh. He loved the sound, especially since there had been a time after his father's death when he'd feared he would never hear it again.

"How about if I come by now and bring some pastries with me?" he offered. "That way at dinner I will not have so many questions to answer and we can have a relaxing visit."

"Suit yourself."

Despite Lucia's seeming indifference, he knew she was pleased. He also knew he would be pumped for answers promptly upon his arrival. Most would center on his love life. Not surprisingly, his mother thought he should be settling down. Even as he thought about Astrid and the relationship that had just ended, his gaze was drawn back down the street to where a royal-blue awning yawned over the wide windows at Expressive Gems.

"Ci sono?" His mother's question snapped him back.

"Yes. *Si.* I am here. I will see you soon."

"A presto," she repeated in Italian before hanging up.

For the next couple of weeks, Rachel worked late. She didn't mind the long hours. Besides, it wasn't as if she had a reason to rush home. The house seemed so big and quiet these days, half furnished as it was. Maybe she should get a dog. Or a cat, since she would soon be without a yard.

"Or maybe I should get a life," she muttered aloud, rising from her chair to stretch out the muscles in her back.

Her shoulders ached from hunching forward. She was working on the piece for Tony and was pleased with her progress. So, too, was she pleased with the progress the contractor had made on the upstairs apartment in so short a span of time. It helped that it was the off-season for construction and she had been clear on what she wanted. Already, plans had been drawn up and the framework for closets and the bathroom was under way. Overhead, the sound of hammers echoed. It was costing her extra, but she'd requested that the work not be done during regular business hours out of deference for her clientele. Because of the noise, it took her a minute to realize that someone was knocking on the front display window.

Tony grinned at her from the opposite side of the glass. The weather was more hospitable today. He had no need for a trench coat. In fact, he wasn't wearing a coat at all. Rather, he had on a thick wool sweater that fit snugly over his broad shoulders and chest. He looked plenty warm. Hot, in fact. Rachel broke out in gooseflesh again.

"Mr. Salerno."

"Tony," he stressed.

"I was just thinking about you," Rachel said as she ushered him inside.

Even though it was true, she realized immediately that it was the wrong thing to say. A bedroom smile creased his cheeks and she swore his hazel eyes turned smoky.

"That is exactly what a man hopes to hear from a beautiful woman. Tell me, *carina,* about these thoughts."

Briefly, she considered flirting back. It wasn't only the fact that Tony was a client that stopped her. She was too out of practice.

"I, um, your necklace is almost ready. Did you come by to see it?"

"What if I said I came by to see you?"

She smiled, not sure how to respond. He said things such as this to the women who worked for Rachel, so she knew he didn't mean anything by it. Still, it had her flustered and tongue-tied. A fresh onslaught of hammering started upstairs and saved her.

"*Santo cielo!* What is that racket?"

"I'm having some renovations done."

"You're adding a second story to the shop?"

She shook her head. "Actually, I'm having the bulk of the square footage turned into an apartment, leaving a small storage attic for the shop."

"This is an older building with a lot of charm and a good location, especially for a young professional. You should have no problem finding a renter."

"I already have one lined up." At his raised eyebrows she added. "Me."

Tony pointed toward the ceiling. "You plan to live there?"

"I do. As soon as the renovation is finished, which should be before spring."

"It cannot be very big." He grimaced. "Forgive me. That was rude."

"That's all right. As for the apartment, it doesn't have to be big. It will just be me." She shrugged. "And maybe a cat."

"A cat?" He shook his head. "No. Dogs are much better company."

"Oh? Do you have a dog?" she inquired.

Tony shook his head. "No. Unfortunately. I am away too much of the time to have one now. But I did when I was a boy in Italy. A Bracco pointer." At her puzzled expression, he added, "It is a breed of hunting dog that is quite popular in Europe. My father spent months training the dog to spot game birds."

"So it was a good hunter," she guessed.

"I do not know." A shadow passed over his face. "My father died before he was able to hunt with her."

"Oh. I'm sorry."

The corners of his mouth turned down and he shrugged. "It was a long time ago."

Which she took to mean he didn't want to talk about it. She understood perfectly. Her father had deserted her a long time ago, too, but time hadn't healed that particular wound, not completely anyway.

"Well, dogs need a yard and I won't have one living here. Cats are more independent."

"Which is why dogs make better pets. That is, if companionship is what you seek." Just that quickly, his smile changed from charming to seductive.

"I—I—I really haven't decided on a pet. Just thinking aloud," she explained hastily.

Overhead, the pounding crescendoed, followed by a thud that shook the rafters.

"*Pazzesco!* Is it like this all day long?"

"In the evenings only. I've asked the contractor to save as much of the noisy work as possible for the off-hours. Construction doesn't make for good background music," she added wryly.

"I would have to agree." He glanced toward the ceiling again before turning his gaze on her. "Will you have a design studio up there or will you continue to work on your jewelry down here?"

Rachel frowned. "I guess I hadn't really given that much thought."

Mal hadn't liked her to bring work home, so she'd never followed through with her plans to turn one of the spare bedrooms of their house into a design studio. But she could do that here. It would be her decision. Her choice. She liked knowing that.

"Would you mind showing me the space? If it would not be too much of an imposition, of course. Just to satisfy my curiosity," he added with an innocent smile.

Rachel could find no reason not to grant the request. She wasn't living there yet, so it wasn't as if she were inviting him into her home. Besides, they would have chaperones. Even so, she hesitated.

"It's dusty," she warned with a meaningful glance at his impeccable attire.

Tony, however, was unconcerned and undeterred. "If my clothes get dirty they can be washed."

More likely dry-cleaned, but she shrugged. "All right. Follow me."

She led him to the back room. Just to the right of the rear entrance was a narrow staircase that led to the second story. The treads were made of wood and not covered with a runner. The stain's finish was scratched and worn off completely in the center. Like the rest of the building, they had a lot of years behind them. They creaked and groaned as Rachel and Tony started up them.

"How old is this building?" Tony wanted to know.

"It dates to the late 1880s. It started out as a mercantile, and it was a card shop before I bought it. Rumor has it that the downstairs was a speakeasy during Prohibition." She sent a smile over her shoulder. Tony was studying her butt. Despite being caught in the act, he smiled.

"A checkered past. I like that. It lends a little spice."

She nearly tripped on a tread. His hands went to her waist immediately, staying a little longer than she thought necessary. "I s-suppose."

They reached the top. A heavy plastic tarp cordoned off the work site in the hope of keeping as much of the sawdust upstairs as possible. Even so, the air was thick with it. She sneezed. Tony offered her a neatly folded square of linen from his pocket. It was monogrammed with his initials and seemed too pretty to wipe her nose, but she did so as discreetly as possible. Rachel tucked the handkerchief into the pocket of her pants. She would have it laundered before returning it.

"Of course, the late 1880s would be considered modern in parts of Italy," he remarked conversationally.

"That's one of the things I admire about Europe. All of that lovely old architecture and so much of it has been preserved. My goal with this renovation is to keep as much of the original finishes and charm of the building as possible, but safety and modern conveniences are a priority, too."

"Form and function."

"Exactly. The previous owner did some updating before I bought the building, but the electrical, plumbing and ventilation systems will need to be modified to accommodate an apartment."

She reached for the tarp, but Tony pulled it aside for her and waved her ahead of him.

"When the work is complete, the entrance to the apartment will be reconfigured so that it will be accessible from outside the store. The original stairs will lead to a storage unit here." She pointed to the right where boxes of varying shapes and sizes were protected under more plastic sheeting.

"Eventually, once I no longer have need for it, I plan to rent out the apartment."

"Any thought on where you would like to live?" he asked.

"Not really. Except that I'll want a house again."

"For your dog." He smiled.

She laughed. "For my dog. Still, this and a cat are a good solution in the interim. And I certainly can't complain about my commute time."

In addition to the hammering, a radio blared vintage rock. The workers stopped what they were doing when they spied her and Tony. There were three of them, all of them outfitted in denim and T-shirts whose holes and wear patterns were the result of serious labor rather than fashion.

"Hey, Mrs. Palmer. Sorry we're making so much noise," the crew's foreman, Will Daniels, said after switching off the tunes. "We should be done with the framing by the weekend, if it's any consolation."

"Oh, that's not a problem, Will. My…um, client, Mr. Salerno, was curious about the layout, so I brought him up to see. I hope that's all right?"

"Yeah. Sure." He rested a pair of meaty hands on his hips. "Me and the guys were thinking about knocking off for fifteen anyway."

"Thanks."

Tony stepped forward and stuck out a hand. "I am Tony, by the way."

The foreman seemed a little surprised. He wiped his palm on the leg of his jeans before shaking Tony's hand.

"Will Daniels." He hooked a thumb over his shoulder. "And these are two of the best framers in the business."

Tony shook each of their hands in turn before glancing around. "There is much to do here, but I see the potential." To Rachel, he said, "It is bigger than I thought it would be, even cutting off a portion for storage."

"The ten-foot ceilings help, as does the fact it is so open," Rachel said.

"Will it remain that way?"

"Pretty much. It's going to be a studio apartment when they're finished."

"Can you show me around?"

His smile was too charming to refuse. While the workers opened their waters and stood a discreet distance away, Rachel walked Tony through the room, her imagination turning studs and subflooring into a finished, furnished and, most importantly, a highly colorful and textural, home.

"This is going to be the kitchen. It's small, but it will have everything I, and whoever the tenant is after me, will need." She pointed to an outside wall. "The sink will be under the window, with cabinetry on either side."

"The finish for the cabinetry?"

"Cherry. I like the richness of the wood."

He made a humming sound. "And the brick, will you leave it exposed?"

"In a section of the main living space, yes. I love the look of it, but for insulation purposes, I'm going to have the rest covered in drywall. Otherwise my heating bill will be through the roof."

"A practical compromise, then."

"Yes."

He followed her to the far wall, where a couple of tall windows faced south.

"The light here would be ideal for a work area." He motioned with his hands as he continued. "It could accommodate a desk here and some storage cabinets there. You could make use of the vertical space by putting in shelving."

Rachel felt her creative juices begin to flow just thinking about it. She could picture the work area Tony was talking about. She liked it...with a little tweaking, of course. With a finger pressed to her lips, she turned in a semicircle.

Half to herself, she said, "I guess I could skimp on the master closet to free up more floor space."

"Am I in your bedroom, *signorina?*"

Ridiculously, she felt her face heat as she watched Tony's mouth curve. Oh, she knew *that* smile.

"Actually, you're in my closet, right about where I was planning to put my shoes."

He was undeterred.

"Do you have any stilettos, *carina?* In red perhaps?"

"Sorry. None."

He made a *tsk*ing sound. "You need to buy some. They do wonderful things for a woman's legs."

"I'll take that under advisement."

"And now?" He stepped toward her, close enough that she could smell his cologne. "Where am I standing now?"

They were where her bed would be. When she said nothing, Tony chuckled softly. "You will look lovely here in the morning light."

The air backed up in her lungs. It took a moment, but

she managed to exhale. Pointing to the right, she said, "The bathroom."

"Hmm?"

"The bathroom. It will go here." She stepped to where the construction crew had already framed in the walls with two-by-fours.

Tony wasn't smiling. In fact, he was frowning. "But there is not enough room here for a proper tub."

"It will have a shower only," Rachel agreed on a sigh. What woman didn't like the indulgence of a long, languid soak?

"You are always welcome at my home. I have a big tub." That sinful smile spread over his face once again when he added, "Big enough to accommodate two."

He was just flirting, she reminded herself. He didn't mean anything by the words. Even so, she wanted to be sure he understood one thing clearly. She didn't condone cheating. Having been the one cheated on, she wasn't about to turn around and become the other woman, even if Tony and Astrid weren't married or, for all she knew, exclusive. She turned to face him and said pointedly, "Perhaps you should be inviting Astrid to join you, then."

"Astrid." He studied the ceiling a moment as if considering, then shook his head. "Astrid and I are no longer seeing one another."

Rachel knew her mouth was gaping open, but it took her a moment to snap it closed after mumbling, "Oh."

"Yes. Oh." He tapped her nose.

Was he laughing at her? Rachel decided to concentrate on business. Did he still want the necklace? "Is this a recent development?"

"Not really. We said our official goodbyes in Stockholm."

"But that was—"

"Prior to me returning to the States. Yes."

"Oh. I'm sorry." She flushed even though he hardly looked broken up about the relationship's demise.

He didn't shrug, but his words were the verbal equivalent when he said, "We enjoyed one another while it lasted, although never in my bathtub. These things happen."

"Yes, they do." Rachel's tone was sharper than she intended.

This time, it was Tony who apologized. "That was an insensitive remark given your current circumstances."

"At least you didn't cheat on her," Rachel replied without thinking.

"I never cheat, *carina*. Never."

She wasn't sure she believed him. Regardless, he wasn't the sort of man who settled down. He was...the perfect rebound. She sucked in a breath and tried to shoo away the thought.

"Is everything all right?"

"Fine. I...I'm just surprised about the necklace. I assumed it was for a special occasion."

"It is. A parting gift as well as a way to wish her luck with her career."

"That's very generous of you." And no doubt it would ensure Astrid went on her way without any fuss or acrimony.

He did shrug this time. "I can afford to be generous. Because that is the case, women want things."

Rachel frowned. "I'm offended on behalf of my gender."

"Everyone wants something, *carina*."

His level gaze left Rachel to wonder exactly what Tony wanted from her.

CHAPTER THREE

"THE house has been sold?" Stunned, Rachel plunked down in the chair in her office. The leather seat groaned even as she did.

On the other end of the telephone line, her real-estate agent, Flora LaBelle, was saying, "I'm just as surprised as you are. Of course, technically, both you and Mal have to accept the offer in order for the sale to go through, but I think you should. It's a pretty decent one, especially for this soft market."

"How decent? Full asking price?"

"Well, no. A little less than that."

"By how much?"

Flora cleared her throat. "By about ten thousand dollars give or take a few hundred."

"Oh." And *damn!* This was not what Rachel wanted to hear. She'd hoped to get as close to the asking price as possible since she would have to split the equity with Mal. She needed every penny.

Flora wasn't done. "The buyer also wants you to pick up the closing costs."

That would be several thousand dollars more out of pocket. "Gee, is that all?"

Despite Rachel's sarcastic tone, Flora continued. "And

the buyer is requesting that all of the kitchen appliances stay with the house."

"The appliances? They're brand new." Indeed, stainless-steel beauties that Rachel had picked out herself just before learning of Mal's infidelity. "I was hoping to keep those."

She and Mal had agreed on that in the settlement. Rachel had planned on them for the apartment's kitchen to keep down the renovation costs.

Flora sighed. "You can buy new appliances, Rachel. I have other listings that have been on the market for months without so much as a nibble. You would be foolish to quash the sale over appliances."

"Can't we at least counter the offer?"

"Mal doesn't want to," Flora said.

"Mal? You've already talked to Mal?"

"I... Yes."

"And he doesn't want to at least see if we can get out of paying the closing costs?"

"He thinks the offer is fair."

Which put the ball back in her court.

Flora was saying, "It could be months before another offer comes along, and even then it might not be as good as this one. It's hard to say which direction the market is heading, Rachel. In the meantime, you'll be making mortgage payments and the winter taxes are coming due. And Mal said the furnace is getting old."

"I get it," Rachel said, figuratively throwing up her hands in defeat. It was a game of roulette, one with a high cover. She couldn't afford to take the risk.

"On the bright side, the buyer has agreed to forego a home inspection and take the house as is."

"Thank God for small miracles. So, what do I need to do now?"

"I can swing by your shop in half an hour for you to sign the purchase agreement. Then I'll get all of the other paperwork in order."

"Terrific," she muttered. "Assuming the sale goes through, how long before we close?"

Flora coughed again. Rachel was coming to dread the sound. "That's another thing. The buyer is in a hurry to take possession."

"Well, I'm *not* in a hurry to leave. My place here won't be ready for months." Rachel knew it was too optimistic to hope she had that long. "Any chance I can pay rent until I can move in here?"

"Sorry, but no."

Rachel cursed silently. "Okay, what are we looking at?"

"Two weeks."

"Two weeks!" This time she cursed out loud. "I can't do two weeks, Flora. Two months would be pushing it."

"That's the buyer's terms, I'm afraid. And it's non-negotiable."

Rachel kneaded her brow. It was quiet overhead at the moment, but the shop was set to close in half an hour and the work crew would arrive. They'd accomplished a lot in the week since she and Tony had walked through her future home, but it would be weeks, months before the apartment was habitable.

"I know it's unusual for a sale to close so quickly, but the buyer is preapproved for the loan and everything else is in order," Flora said. "Of course, any additional costs in expediting the matter—courier service and things of that nature—will be borne by the buyer."

"It's about time they offered to pay something," Rachel muttered.

"I'll be by shortly with the papers," Flora said.

Rachel barely heard her. Her house was sold. Where was she supposed to live until the apartment was ready?

The days ticked by even as she sought an answer to that question. Finally, all that remained between her and a date with a moving van was the weekend. Late in the afternoon on Friday, she paced the house from the all-white kitchen to the quiet bedrooms and then back down the hall to the living room. Out front, the For Sale sign her Realtor had staked on the leaf-scattered lawn bore the addition of a bright red SOLD! sticker. Rachel studied the sign as she cupped a mug of green tea in her chilled hands. As eager as she was to leave, she wasn't ready to go.

She sipped the tea, swallowing it around the lump of dread in her throat. She'd boxed up some of her things, items she wouldn't need right away. They were at the shop now, wedged into every nook and cranny she could spare. But that was about all she had accomplished. She hated moving, even if she wasn't going to miss the house itself. Turning away from the window, she glanced around. Everything here was so beige and benign. All of the rooms were a study in monochromic understatement. She preferred a more eclectic decor—bursts of color, texture and pattern. But none of that was reflected here. *She* wasn't reflected here. And that was her fault. She'd demurred to Mal's sedate preferences to avoid argument and to keep the peace that her parents' marriage had lacked.

Indeed, the house as a whole was a compromise. If it had been up to her, she and Mal would have lived in a rambling, restored farmhouse just outside of town. He'd vetoed that idea as soon as she'd brought it up, just after their wedding. Too much upkeep and too far from the city, he'd said. No, the newly built story-and-a-half in the Sherwood Forrest subdivision was the way to go. It was in an excellent school district, close to parks and shopping, and, as such, a better investment overall. Knowing what it had just sold for, Rachel wasn't so sure.

Regardless, Monday would be here before she was ready for it if she didn't get busy.

"So, what is Plan B going to be?" she murmured.

Her sister had offered the use of her one-bedroom apartment's futon, and Rachel knew she would be welcome at her mother's condominium. Neither option held any appeal, even as a last resort.

Taking up residence in the small, pink-walled room that still sported the canopy bed of her girlhood felt too much like taking a step backward. As for her sister's closet-size apartment, Rachel needed more privacy than a bed in the living room would afford. Heidi's lifestyle reflected her age and single status. She had a crazy work schedule and an active social life, which meant she came and went at all hours of the day. Besides, Rachel didn't think her back could stand more than a night on the lumpy futon.

Her cell phone trilled as she made herself a second cup of tea.

"Promise not to hate me," Heidi beseeched as soon as Rachel answered.

It was never a good sign when her sister started off a conversation that way. Rachel promised anyway.

"I told Dad about your divorce and housing situation."

"Dad?" Rachel was too busy being surprised to be angry. "When and where did you see him?"

The last time their paths had crossed was two Christmases prior, when he'd moved back to the area after a year of selling real estate in Florida. A perfect occupation for him, Rachel had thought. If anyone could sell undesirable swamp land for top dollar, it would be Griff

Preston. He'd promised to stay in touch. He hadn't. No surprise there.

"Today. I ran into him at work of all places. He came in for lunch and sat in my section." Heidi waited tables and sometimes tended bar at a private golf club. Even when the course was closed for the season, the clubhouse remained a favorite hangout for the CEO set and other business people. "He didn't even recognize me at first."

Her sister laughed. That was Heidi's way. Live and let live. Rachel, however, fumed on her behalf. What kind of father didn't recognize his own daughter?

"Was he alone?" she asked before she could remind herself that she didn't care.

"He was with a woman."

Again, no surprise. Their father had left their mother for someone else, although he'd never remarried. That initial affair hadn't lasted long, but over the years he'd never wanted for female companionship. The older he grew, the younger and tackier the women he dated became.

"Let's see. Thirties and blonde?" Rachel inquired blithely as she dunked the tea bag in a mug of boiling water.

"Nope. A redhead this time, and I think she might be younger than you."

Rachel shifted the phone to her other ear and began dunking the tea bag more vigorously. Mal, Tony and now her father. Was every man on the planet dating a woman who was younger than she was?

"Any tattoos?"

"A red rose on the back of her neck and some other designs that I couldn't make out poking from the cuffs of her blouse. I'm betting there are more. Obviously her mother never gave her the lecture our mom gave us."

"Anything on your hip at twenty will be sliding down your backside at fifty and you don't even want to know where it will end up by the time you're seventy," Rachel recited. They both laughed.

"So, you're not mad?" Heidi asked.

"I don't like him knowing my business," Rachel said slowly. "He lost that right a long time ago."

Rachel knew that, generally speaking, Heidi agreed with the sentiment, but Heidi's feeling were that if showering his daughters with gifts or money now and again eased Griff's guilt, so be it. Take whatever he offered. He owed them that much.

"He's going to be calling you," Heidi said.

"Why?" She gritted her teeth to keep from following up the question with the slew of unflattering adjectives popping around in her head.

"He has a friend who owns a condo development. The bank foreclosed on one of the units a couple of months ago and the guy bought it back for a song. It's sitting empty until they can do some updating and put it back on the market. You wouldn't even have to pay—"

"No," she said flatly.

"No? Why not, Rachel? It solves your most pressing problem," Heidi said. "If you won't stay with me or Mom, you'll have to pay rent somewhere else until the apartment over your shop is ready."

As it was, Rachel just barely could afford the contractor she'd hired, though she comforted herself with the thought that it made more sense in the long run to add an income property than to pay rent. Now, she was going to have to move twice and pay rent somewhere in the interim, too.

Still, Rachel was adamant. "I don't want Dad's help."

"That doesn't mean you can't take advantage of it... and him," Heidi said. "If he wants to help, I say let him."

"Did he say anything about my divorce?" When her sister remained silent, Rachel prompted, "Well?"

"Just that he wasn't surprised." Heidi coughed. "He said he knew from the start that Mal wasn't the right sort of man for you."

She hated that Griff was right. She'd known her relationship with Mal was far from perfect even before he was unfaithful, but it had seemed far more perfect than her parents' marriage. Men like her father cheated. Flashy men who were quick with compliments. Sexy men who were steeped in charm. Tony Salerno sprang to mind. Men like that couldn't settle down. They liked adventure, variety. They broke hearts along with their promises. But men like Mal? He'd seemed so safe.

He worked as a financial adviser. He wore conservative suits. He drove a midsize sedan the color of sand. He was solid, dependable—boring, according to Heidi. But Rachel had craved boring after all of their father's drama.

"Like Dad is such an expert on marriage and relationships," she said drily.

"You know Dad."

Rachel was far from mollified. "He barely knows Mal. He barely knows me. Or you, for that matter."

Griff and Mal had met only twice—the day of Rachel's wedding and that Christmas when her father had popped in unexpectedly, about as welcome as the heavy loaf of store-bought fruitcake he'd brought with him.

"You know what? It doesn't matter."

"Rach—"

"I don't want his help." Good and worked up now with righteous indignation, Rachel exclaimed, "In fact, I'd sooner strike a bargain with the devil than take it."

Her phone beeped. Another call was coming in. "I've got to go, Heidi. I'll talk to you later."

She was relieved to end the conversation with her

sister until she heard Tony's deep voice. The devil, it turned out, was on her other line.

"Good evening, Rachel."

"Mr. Salerno."

"Tony." She heard a soft chuckle. Then, "I apologize for calling after hours and on a Friday no less."

Rachel gave out her cell number only to select customers. Tony was one of the few, due to the amount of money he'd spent at Expressive Gems over the years.

"That's all right. Is there a problem?"

"That depends on you. I've had a change in my itinerary. I was planning to pick up the necklace on Wednesday. Unfortunately, I need to return to New York before then."

"So, you want to pick it up early."

"I do. If it is ready."

"I finished it just this afternoon. I think you'll be pleased with the result."

"That goes without saying. Your work is always exceptional, which is why I keep coming back."

"Thank you. I can open the shop early tomorrow." Normally on Saturdays, she didn't flip the sign on the door until ten o'clock. Expressive Gems was closed on Sundays, as were most of the shops downtown except for the bakery and restaurants.

He made a humming noise. "I was hoping I could pick it up tonight. I will pay you extra for your trouble, of course."

"Oh, it's no trouble." Rachel's response was automatic, that of a businesswoman. The customer was always right, especially a customer with pockets as deep as Tony's. But she also thought it might do her good to get out of the house for a while, even if only to go back to the shop where she'd already spent the bulk of her day.

They made plans to meet in an hour, which gave her enough time to change her clothes, freshen up her makeup and do something more flattering with the hair she'd pulled back in a messy ponytail upon arriving home. She settled on a French braid, and traded in the comfortable black yoga pants and a T-shirt for a pair of khakis and a navy blue knit sweater with three-quarter-length sleeves. Tony was waiting in the parking lot behind Expressive Gems when she arrived. He was wearing a tuxedo.

"I feel underdressed," she remarked on a self-conscious laugh as she unlocked the door and tapped the deactivation code into the security system's panel.

He glanced down, as if just realizing that he was garbed in black formalwear and French cuffs. "I was at a fund-raiser for the Detroit Institute of Art. I was asked to introduce the guest of honor, after which I was able to slip away."

"It must have just started."

"I will not be missed," he replied on a shrug.

She wasn't sure she agreed. Looking as he did, he would have had the attention of every woman in the building. Add in his charisma and business savvy, and men would have wanted to seek him out, too.

Tony was saying, "I hope I did not take you away from anything too important this evening."

She almost laughed. Summoning up a bit of self-deprecating humor, she replied, "Important? No. I was at a party. A pity party. Guest of honor. Believe me, I was happy for the interruption."

"A pity party." He frowned.

"I was feeling sorry for myself," she clarified. "Wallowing."

"English may be my second language, but I am familiar with the term." He stepped behind her, helping her out of the coat she'd begun to slip off. She felt his breath graze her temple when he continued. "I have a hard time picturing you wallowing."

"I assure you, I can do a credible job of it when I put my mind to it."

"*Allora*... What is the reason for this pity party?"

"My house has sold, and I have until Monday to be out."

"But the apartment upstairs cannot be ready so soon." Tony nodded then. "Ah. I see. It is not ready. What will you do?"

"I'm weighing my options."

Tony studied Rachel. From the way her mouth tightened, he decided none of them was to her liking.

"If I may be so bold, what are those options?"

"Oh, the usual. I can go and live with family. My mother and sister have already made the obligatory offer. I also could…" She shook her head and added resolutely, "No. I won't even consider the condo."

"Why is this condo not worthy of consideration?"

Rachel blinked. It was clear she didn't realize that she'd shared that last part with him.

"Sorry. I was thinking aloud. It's just that my father, well, apparently he has a business associate who owns a condo where I could live rent-free for a few months."

"But you will not even consider it. Why?" Tony asked curiously.

She sighed. "It's complicated. My father and I are not on the best of terms."

"Ah." That was all Tony said. He found that the less one prodded, the more some people opened up. Sure enough, after another sigh, Rachel started talking.

"When it comes right down to it, I barely know him— my father." She snorted out what passed for a laugh. "I can count on one hand the number of times I've seen him in the past half-dozen years."

"He and your mother are divorced."

"Since I was a little girl. My sister was practically a baby when he left us."

Rachel's tone was matter-of-fact, but her expression was wounded. Interestingly, she appeared more broken up over her parents' failed marriage than she did her own.

"There was another woman," Tony guessed.

"That's right." Her laughter was humorless. "And I thought Mal would be safe."

"What do you mean by that?"

"Never mind." She worked up a smile. "That was just a little more wallowing on my part. See, I told you I was good at it."

Tony wasn't ready to let her previous remark go just yet. "Instead of trying to remain safe, maybe you need to be reckless every now and then. Take more chances."

"I'm not a fan of taking chances."

"I think you are." He stepped closer. "You are a businesswoman. That involves risk."

"True, but—"

"And you are an artist. Again, you are putting yourself on the line."

Her brow furrowed, leaving Tony with the distinct impression he'd struck a chord. But then Rachel was shaking her head. "Let me clarify, I am not a fan of taking chances when it comes to personal relationships."

He nodded slowly. "It is much harder to put one's self at risk emotionally, and that is what relationships require."

"Are you going to tell me you're speaking from experience?" Her expression was droll.

Tony laughed softly. "I confess. I am a far better teacher than student when it comes to such matters."

"I hope I won't offend you, but I don't think there is anything you could teach me when it comes to relationships."

He smiled even as she blushed.

"Nothing?" He had the advantage and they both knew it. Tony took another step forward. Her back was literally to the wall.

"Y-your track record with women says as much."

"Simply because a relationship does not end with me getting down on bended knee, does not make it a failure."

"What does that make it?"

He shrugged and pushed away the thought that he might be missing something, denying himself something less obvious than permanence.

"I enjoy myself. The woman I am with enjoys herself. It lasts as long as it lasts. There are no hurt feelings. No repercussions." He leaned one forearm on the wall. He lowered his head, lowered his voice to a seductive whisper. "When was the last time you *enjoyed* yourself, *signorina?*"

Her blush was telling, but when she spoke, her tone was so professional that he was left to marvel at her control... and fantasize about breaking it.

"I think we've gotten off track here, Tony. Let's see about that necklace."

Off track or not, she was finally calling him by his given name. Tony straightened and backed up a couple of steps. Very well. He had pushed her far enough, especially since he had no idea where he wanted her to go in the end.

"Yes, the necklace. I am eager to see it."

Rachel turned and nearly tripped over a row of boxes that was lined up against the wall on the other side of her office door. If not for his hands on her waist, she would have fallen.

"What is all of this?" he asked once her balance was restored.

He needn't have asked. The boxes bore labels such as Extra Linens, Holiday Decorations and Board Games.

"Just some items I came across while clearing out my closets. I thought some of my employees might be able to use them." She frowned as she studied the boxes. "It's amazing the amount of stuff you accumulate over the years."

She continued to the safe then. After getting out the necklace, she took it to one of the display cases, where she draped it on a headless black-velvet-covered bust.

Her expression was a mixture of pride and apprehension. Oh, she was a true artist, all right. And from his experience, artists were a passionate lot.

"Well, what do you think?" she prodded, and it occurred to him that he'd been staring, not at the necklace but at Rachel.

He redirected his gaze. The aquamarine was surrounded by smaller stones and set in platinum filigree. Under the overhead lights, it took on an almost ethereal quality.

"It is exquisite," Tony remarked. "You have outdone yourself, Rachel."

Her smile was genuine and he enjoyed seeing it.

"Thank you."

"Astrid will love it."

"It is gorgeous enough to soothe a broken heart," she mused. Then she blanched. "That was rude of me. Please accept my apology."

"There is nothing to forgive. As I told you, no hearts were broken."

"Shall I gift wrap this?" she asked as she placed the necklace in a box that bore the shop's logo.

Tony reached inside the breast pocket of his tuxedo jacket and pulled out his wallet. "No. I will handle that."

A moment later they were at the shop's back door with Rachel once again setting the alarm, when he asked, "Have you eaten dinner? I was thinking of stopping at Carlo's for a steak."

"Steak?" she repeated.

"They serve other things, if you do not care for red meat."

"It's not that. I like red meat."

"But you've eaten already." Tony adjusted his cuff and glanced at the gold watch strapped to his wrist.

"Actually, I haven't." She frowned. "I never even had lunch today."

"Then let me buy you dinner," he offered as they crossed the parking lot. "To celebrate."

"What exactly are we celebrating?"

Her expression turned leery when he replied, "I am sure we will think of something."

CHAPTER FOUR

RACHEL wasn't sure she trusted the gleam in Tony's eyes, but she agreed to have dinner with him. She reminded herself that Tony was a valued client. She was sure that, as big a flirt as he was, he didn't consider dinner with her to be an actual date.

Still, Rachel had to admit it did wonders for her battered ego when they walked into the restaurant and every woman in the place, even a couple who were old enough to be his mother, gave him the once-over as the pair of them followed the maître d' to their table.

"You attract a lot of attention," she remarked with a wry grin.

He glanced about as they took their seats. Either he was oblivious or he had simply grown accustomed to the appreciative stares he instigated among members of the opposite sex.

"It is the tuxedo. It makes me look important." He picked up the wine list. As he scanned it, he continued, "People dress so casually these days. If not for weddings or occasions such as this evening's fundraiser, most men would never bother with jackets and ties, much less something this formal."

"And women wouldn't bother with skirts or high heels," Rachel agreed, uncomfortably aware that she was wearing neither. But then how could she have known Tony would show up outfitted in Armani and invite her to dinner?

"As a man who appreciates beautiful things, I find myself grateful that women appear to be far more willing to dress up than men are."

"I used to be," she said slowly. But Mal hadn't cared for her fashion choices. Too bold. Too flashy. Just as with their home decor, he preferred understated, demure. Rachel smoothed the linen napkin over her lap. Was she really wearing cotton khakis and a pair of penny loafers? She cleared her throat. "You don't seem to mind dressing up."

"That is Luigi's doing. My tailor," he supplied before she could ask. "He has clothed me from the time I celebrated my First Holy Communion in the second grade to the tuxedo I am wearing tonight. His clothes fit well. As a result, they are comfortable."

"Does this Luigi live in Italy?"

"He does. I am faithful to him."

An interesting word choice, Rachel thought.

Tony was saying, "I appreciate anything that is made with care and craftsmanship, whether it comes from a tailor in Rome or from a very talented jewelry designer in Rochester, Michigan."

Their waiter arrived with a pair of menus. After introducing himself and explaining the evening's specials, he took their beverage orders and retreated.

Rachel reverted to small talk. "So, you're leaving town again. Are you heading to New York or abroad?"

"New York, for a couple of days at least. Then it will be on to Italy. There is a vineyard there that I'm profiling for one of the magazines."

No weary sighs sounded after he finished listing his itinerary. It was just another month in the life of a wealthy media mogul.

"You enjoy traveling."

"What is not to enjoy, *carina?* The world is a big place. I prefer to see it, experience it, rather than merely read about it."

"Even in magazines such as the ones you own?" she asked.

"The majority of the people who read our magazines are interested in seeing the places we feature."

She tucked away a wisp of hair that had come loose from her braid. "The minority then are more like me, living vicariously."

"Surely, as one who designs jewelry, you travel."

"Sometimes, yes. But such trips are mainly intended to exploit business opportunities and for networking purposes. It's not the same as traveling for leisure."

"You must take time for yourself, time for pleasure." His accent gave the last word a seductive edge that pulled her back to his earlier question. When was the last time she'd enjoyed herself? The double entendre in both cases was intentional, she was sure.

For some reason, rather than feeling the need to retreat, this time it made her bold. "I plan to. In fact, I would like to visit your homeland."

"Have you ever been to Italy?"

"To Rome for a couple of days with friends just after we graduated from college. We backpacked through five countries in two weeks."

Her father had tried to pay her airfare. A graduation gift, Griff had claimed in a letter, since he was unable to make it to the commencement ceremony. She'd torn up both the impersonal missive and the check. When it came time for Heidi to graduate, he'd made the same offer. Heidi accepted without hesitation and used the money she saved to spend a weekend in a swanky hotel on the French

Riviera. The memory still irked. Rachel said now, "It was a long time ago."

"The next trip you will enjoy other cities," he said. "When you are in Italy, in addition to another visit to Rome, you must experience Florence and Venice, of course. Milan, too. I would be happy to act as your tour guide."

He winked and selected a fat slice of bread, which he slathered with a decadent amount of creamy butter. Her mouth began to water, the result, she assured herself, of the combination of carbohydrates and fat, rather than other forbidden treats. After swallowing a bite, he said, "I will tell you all of the best places to eat and stay."

"That's kind of you," she replied politely. She doubted she could afford any of the places he would suggest. Still, the conversation had her thinking. She was due a vacation. "I've always wanted to see Venice," she murmured.

"Because of the glass artists," he guessed.

She nodded. She shouldn't be surprised that he understood. "I've used Murano beads in my work on occasion. The vibrant colors are always well received."

"Yet you've never been to Venice." He shook his head. "You must make time for yourself. Time for yourself and for your craft. Creativity such as yours must be fed."

Whether he was being kind or not, she agreed. Reality, however, spoiled her mood. "I'm afraid a trip to Italy or anywhere else is a long way off. Most of my time and resources have been put into my business and that will continue to be the case."

He set the bread aside and blotted his mouth with a napkin. "Is this your dream, Rachel? Owning your shop and dabbling in design while you mainly sell the work of other people?"

She hadn't expected the question, so she wasn't sure how to answer it. "I love my shop," she began.

"But is it your passion, Rachel? Is it your dream?" he asked a second time.

Her dream? She shook her head. It was a bit of a shock to admit, "Owning the shop is what allows me to dream. But being a shopkeeper isn't my dream."

"Designing jewelry, *that* is your passion." His smile was self-satisfied. "You owe it to yourself to pursue that passion full force."

Spoken like a man with the resources to pursue any and all passions.

"It's not as simple as that, I'm afraid."

"It can be, *carina*." It was a curious thing to say, but before she could ask Tony what he meant, he was saying, "Have you always wanted to be a jewelry designer?"

"Yes and no. I was always sketching ideas in a notebook, but when I went to college, I decided it was smarter to major in finance." That was how she'd met Mal. They'd worked at the same bank, which had been her first job post graduation. It was impossible not to think about how different her life might be right now had she followed her heart where her career was concerned.

"An artist with a head for numbers," Tony noted.

"Yes. I was being practical." Her lips puckered on the word. "I had student loans to repay, and I was determined to have my own place even though my mother said I could move back in." She laughed humorlessly. "Gee, a decade later and I'm facing the same choice."

The waiter arrived with their drinks and another basket of warm bread. Tony had ordered a glass of pinot noir. She'd gone with unsweetened iced tea. Before taking a sip, she squeezed in the juice from a wedge of lemon.

When she glanced up, Tony was frowning.

"So, you have nowhere to go."

"That's being a little dramatic. I'll be fine."

Tony and Rachel chatted throughout their meal on a wide range of topics. All the while, an idea festered in much the same way the irritation of a grain of sand produced a pearl. Still, Tony pushed the idea to the back of his mind, as was his way. He preferred to stew over things, let them simmer. As a businessman, not rushing blindly forward had saved him millions of dollars and countless headaches. This idea could be strictly business, though it carried a tempting personal element, making it all the more vital that he proceed with caution.

He liked Rachel. She struck him as smart and level-headed. He respected her immensely, even if he'd never quite been able to figure her out. From what he knew of her, he decided she would be the last person to consider herself a mystery, yet she was to him. A very attractive mystery hidden beneath a tidy, unobtrusive exterior.

Tony had always wondered if perhaps it was Rachel's primness, coupled with her off-limits status as a married woman, that piqued his interest. Now, she was no longer wed, so part of the equation didn't add up. Still, his curiosity was far from satisfied. If anything, it was amplified.

She was an artist, ridiculously gifted and creative, with an eye for both beauty and detail. Her work proved as much. To his mind, her genius was wasted in her small shop. With the right backing and connections, she could make a name for herself in New York, London or Rome.

In his travels, Tony had made the acquaintance of a lot of artists who dabbled in an array of mediums. He'd interviewed them. He'd dated them. He'd almost married one. They tended to be moody, eclectic, flamboyant and highly sexual. Outwardly, at least, Rachel was none of those things. She dressed like an accountant, simple and streamlined. No flounces or ruffles. No frills of any sort. She barely wore jewelry, other than a simple wedding band and even that was now absent. He'd seen her in a skirt exactly once. Its hem had hit midcalf and the flat shoes she'd paired with it had done nothing for the glimpse of legs he'd seen.

The woman came across as repressed, sexually and otherwise. That made her a challenge as well as an enigma. He liked challenges, too.

"Is something wrong with your steak, Tony?"

It took him a moment to realize that during his musings he'd been staring at the perfectly cooked porterhouse while she'd been eating.

"No. It is excellent." He cut off a chunk as if to prove the point and popped it into his mouth. The prime cut of seasoned meat melted like butter on his tongue. He washed it down with some wine, a decent vintage, although he'd had better. He motioned with the tines of his fork. "And your fish? How is it?"

"Delicious," she said of the grilled sea bass.

They couldn't be more different. Even their entrees told him as much. He'd gone for red meat cooked rare and smothered in sautéed mushrooms and caramelized onions with a side of creamy mashed potatoes. It was decadence on a plate. Meanwhile, she'd selected fish, grilled rather than pan fried, and flaked with herbs in place of any sort of sauce. Steamed broccoli florets and a fluffy rice pilaf finished off the plate. Repressed, he thought again. Even her food choices showed restraint.

But then she surprised him.

"Would you mind if I tried a bite of your steak?"

The request was as unexpected as the color that rose in her cheeks afterward.

"Of course."

He started to slice off a generous piece with the intention of setting it on her plate, but then he downsized to a bite-size portion, which he offered to her on his fork. He smiled as he issued his dare. Adam was tempting Eve with the apple this time. Would she?

Rachel's acquiescence was all the more thrilling because of the hesitation that preceded it. She wasn't one to be led blindly into temptation. But neither was she too straitlaced to accept a dare. He'd claimed a victory of sorts.

"Ooh, that's good." Even though there was no need, she dabbed her mouth with her napkin. He liked her lips, the top one in particular. "There's nothing like a good steak."

"Then why didn't you order one?"

Her eyelids flickered in surprise. "I…I like fish."

"For its taste or for its Omega-3 fatty acids and all of the heart-healthy hype associated with it?" he challenged.

"Both." Her brow furrowed. "It doesn't need to be either-or."

"We agree there. I enjoy fish. But when I want a steak, I order a steak. I see no point in denying myself." He cut off another piece and popped it in his mouth.

"I guess that's where we differ," she replied. "I see no point in overindulging."

"Is it overindulgence, I wonder?" He sipped his wine, pleased when she shifted in her seat under his considering stare. He made her uncomfortable. He liked knowing that, since he was never quite sure of his footing around her. Mysteries made a man wary of where he stepped. "Everything in moderation, no?"

"I suppose."

A little later, when they had finished their meals, the waiter came with the dessert cart. Tony fully expected Rachel to pass. Half of her meal remained on her plate.

Not but a moment earlier, she'd claimed to be full. She darted a glance in his direction before telling the server, "I'd like a slice of the strawberry cheesecake, please, and a cup of coffee."

"The same," Tony said.

When they were alone, she said, "You're wondering why I ordered dessert."

"Why did you?"

"I wanted it."

"You're a quick study, *carina*." Tony laughed, but he couldn't help feeling the joke was on him given the amount of interest her simple statement stirred.

After their meal, they walked to their cars. They'd driven separately from her shop.

"It's been a long day," she commented idly. On a sigh, she added, "A long week."

"Will you be working tomorrow?"

"No." She sighed again and the cold air that floated white around her face seemed to mock her. "Not the way you mean at least. I have to buy more boxes and make a serious dent in my packing. Monday will be here before I'm ready for it." She didn't seem to be talking to him as much as saying her to-do list aloud. "I probably should look into renting a storage unit, too, since I likely won't have room for all of my belongings wherever I wind up."

She laughed; the sound leaned more toward hysteria than hilarity.

Another idea nudged forward. Even as he considered it, she was saying, "Maybe I shouldn't move everything. Maybe I should see if the new owner wants to buy some of the furnishings. They aren't really my style, but I wound up with them in the settlement. Mal got the large-screen plasma television. I got the living-room sofa and chairs."

"It sounds to me like your ex-husband got the better end of the deal."

"What is it with men and huge TVs?"

"Size matters," he said drily.

"Apparently." She smiled up at him. "I don't suppose you know anyone in the market for a really big, really boring beige couch? It's well made. Hardly shows any wear. I'm willing to part with it cheap."

"Not off the top of my head, no. Perhaps you could sell it online," he suggested.

She nodded in consideration. "My mother thinks I should keep it. She says it's better than having no couch at all."

"Perhaps you should listen to her."

"Do you listen to your mother?" she asked.

"It depends on what she is telling me."

"In other words, no."

"If I listened to her, I would be married by now with half a dozen children scampering about my knee."

Rachel shook her head. "Sorry, but I can't picture that."

Tony couldn't see himself settled down with a family either, so it surprised him that her statement bothered him. "I do not seem the fatherly type to you?" he pressed.

"Afraid not. Nor do you strike me as husband material." She stopped. "God! I hope I haven't insulted you."

He shrugged. "The women I date all seem interested in marriage…eventually." Which was why he never let things progress too far. Parting was much easier, not to mention far less messy, when deep emotions weren't involved. He knew that from Kendra. They'd almost made it to the altar. He would never make that mistake again.

"That's because men and women have different agendas where romance is concerned."

He smiled in full agreement. "Indeed we do."

"Back to that couch. I could keep it. Same with the chairs. But they're really not my style." She swung around and poked him in the chest. "Don't."

He held up his hands. "Don't what?"

"Don't ask me why I own furnishings I didn't want in the first place." Her expression sobered. "It's not as simple as that when you're married. It can't always be about you and what you want."

"Rachel—"

She looked angry and oddly defeated. "When you're married, you have to make compromises, Tony."

"Did you make compromises, *carina?* Or did you sell your soul?"

She gasped.

"I apologize," he said, though he wasn't sorry for speaking the truth. "I will not pretend to understand marriage. I am thirty-eight years old, after all, and to my mother's everlasting regret, I have managed to remain unattached."

"But not without regular companionship."

"As I said earlier, I see no reason to deny myself. That applies to women, as well."

"Which is exactly why you're not married." She laughed, taking the sting out of the accusation. Tony laughed, as well.

"Is that the chicken or the egg?" he wondered aloud. "I have never been sure if my fondness for women is the reason I am single or if I am single because I like women." He held up a finger. "For the record, I was tempted to relinquish my bachelorhood once."

It wasn't the sort of thing he admitted to many people, but then Rachel was easy to talk to, and she'd already shared enough of her own private business with him that he felt it only fair.

Rachel stopped walking. "Really? When?"

"Long ago. Back when I was young and romantic."

"I think you are still full of romance."

"Yes?" He smiled encouragingly.

Rachel rolled her eyes. Little by little, that professional veneer of hers was fading. He liked the woman he spied beneath. She had a sense of humor, a warmth that he found every bit as alluring as those lush eyelashes and full lips.

"How long were you together?"

"We met at freshman orientation and dated for all four years of college. She was a fixture at my home. My mother and sister adored her."

"That makes it hard. My mother and sister were never very fond of Mal. Can I ask what happened?"

"Kendra and I had different ideas for our future. I wanted to start the Fortuna Publishing Group. She did not think I needed to work. She gave me back my ring the day I entered talks to buy a small, struggling magazine that has since become Fortuna's flagship publication."

Rachel was quiet a moment. Then Tony felt her hand on his arm. "Her loss."

"The same might be said for your husband, no?"

They reached her car. Rachel turned. Her expression tightened. "He had an affair with his secretary."

"How cliché," Tony replied in lieu of offering actual sympathy. They had been down that road already. She didn't need or want condolences.

"Oh, it gets even more cliché than that." She leaned against the closed car door, arms folded, half of her mouth turned up in a poor facsimile of a smile.

"Ah. This secretary is blonde and younger than you are," Tony guessed. He allowed his gaze to skim down to the small but perfect breasts showcased above her crossed arms. "And more…endowed?"

Rachel didn't appear to notice the direction of his gaze.

"All of the above." She sighed and dropped her arms to her sides. "And apparently I was the last to know. It had been going on for more than a year when I found a receipt."

"For?"

"Jewelry." Her voice rose. "He bought her...jewelry!"

Tony wondered if in that slight hesitation before she'd finished the revelation she'd considered adding an expletive. She certainly would have been entitled. Tony did it for her in his reply.

"The bastard. At least you have the satisfaction of knowing that whatever your ex bought for his mistress, it was far inferior to anything you are capable of creating."

His observation startled a laugh out of her. "Thank you."

"You're gifted, Rachel. I have told you so many times. You need to believe it."

"Thank you," she said again.

Afterward, she glanced down. Was she embarrassed? He reached over to raise her chin. The idea that had been forming spilled out in a whisper.

"I could take you places, *carina.*"

"E-excuse me?"

He smiled, aware of the direction her thoughts had taken. *That, too,* he thought wryly. But for now, they would keep it business.

"I could introduce you to people who could advance your career and see to it that you have a place, a presence among the world's top jewelry designers."

Adam tempting Eve, he thought again, and watched her eyes widen in interest.

"You have thought about this," he guessed.

"Dreamed about it, more like. I...I don't know what to say, Tony."

"Say nothing, then. Just promise me that you will think about it."

"I'll think about it," she repeated slowly.

"Good."

He dropped his hand, but not before running his knuckles along the underside of her jaw. He was used to taking what he wanted. For that matter, he was used to having what he wanted offered to him freely. Maybe that was part of Rachel's appeal, as well. She offered nothing. Yet. He would need to proceed slowly. Eventually, he promised himself, they would be more than what one might call patron and artist. When she was ready, he had no qualms about being her segue back into the dating scene, after which they would part on amicable terms. He and the women he enjoyed always parted on amicable terms. When one made no promises, it was hard to be blamed for not keeping them. For now, he'd given her much to consider.

"Thank you again for dinner."

"You are welcome. The next time, you will order the steak. You cannot have what you want unless you ask for it."

She opened her car door, but then hesitated. Turning toward him, she rose on tiptoe and kissed his cheek. If the look on her face when she pulled back had been solely one of gratitude, Tony might not have pressed his advantage. He captured her lips before she could back away, lingering just long enough to make it clear that his intentions were not purely platonic.

This time, the cool night air mocked him as his breath sawed out, not completely even afterward.

"Buona notte." It wasn't until after he said it that Tony realized he'd slipped into his native Italian. "Good night."

"Have a safe trip." Her smile was polite and back to

being professional when she added, "I hope to see you at Expressive Gems when you get back to the States."

"Count on it."

HER man radar was way off, Rachel concluded as she slipped beneath the covers of her bed that night. That was the only explanation for her reaction to Tony's kiss. He was being kind. He knew she had just come through a rough personal patch. He wasn't interested in her romantically. Outside of business, they had no real relationship.

I could take you places.

Rachel had to admit, the thrill she'd experienced when he'd uttered those words in his seductive accent had been completely unprofessional. Indeed, she couldn't recall the last time she'd experienced that low pull in her belly. The past year she'd lived like a nun as her marriage unraveled and lawyers had picked over the ruins. And, in truth, the past couple of years her sex life had been less than fulfilling, understandable given that Mal had been sleeping with someone else. She might have excused her reaction to Tony based on pent-up need, but it would have been a lie. The truth was she'd always found him sexy and attractive. And, until tonight, off-limits. This evening, however, he hadn't merely flirted with her. As out of practice as she was, he had seemed interested.

I could take you places.

Had he only been speaking to her as an artist when making that claim?

It didn't matter. Her career was what mattered. It was what she intended to focus on now. And so the question that festered was: If he was offering to help her in that regard, could she afford to turn him down?

CHAPTER FIVE

RACHEL was out of bed early the next day, in part because she couldn't sleep. She blamed Tony, her own idiocy and more than a year of celibacy for her restlessness. She decided to put her energy to good use and got busy packing even before the sun was fully up.

She started in the dining room, specifically with the items from inside the china cabinet. She pushed the hair that had escaped her ponytail back from her face and carefully swaddled a blown-glass vase in bubble wrap before placing it in the open box. The vase had been a wedding gift from one of Mal's work colleagues, but the artist in her decided not to hold that against it. The dinnerware, service for eight rimmed with tiny forget-me-nots, however, could go. A few months back, she might have considered smashing every last piece of it, just to be spiteful. She was more practical than that now. She would sell it. The furniture, too. It was foolish to settle for things she didn't like or want, especially now that she no longer had to.

Tony was right. She had sold her soul. Now she was buying it back.

By noon, she was feeling quite proud of herself. Everything she wanted from the dining room had fit into two manageable boxes. The rest was packed up with the contents carefully listed on the outside of the cartons.

She'd called Heidi earlier for help. Her sister was a whiz when it came to selling things on the internet. She'd promised to be over later with her digital camera—Mal had gotten theirs in the settlement—and take photographs of some of the furniture to upload to an online auction site.

"Bring lunch," Rachel had thought to add.

Glancing at her watch now, she wondered what was keeping Heidi. Rachel was starving. The doorbell sounded as she rummaged through the pantry. Eating a handful of cereal right out of the box, she went to answer it.

"I hope you remembered to pick up diet cola," she said, pulling open the door.

Tony stood on the leaf-scattered porch, his expression amused. He spread out his arms. "Sorry. I was not aware I was supposed to bring beverages."

"I thought you were my sister." As if a man as masculine as he was could be mistaken for a woman. "I'm expecting her. She's supposed to bring lunch."

"I promise not to stay long." A gust of wind sent leaves swirling around his ankles. "Would it be all right if I stepped inside?"

"Oh! Of course. Come in."

Rachel backed up, painfully aware of her disheveled appearance. After rolling out of bed that morning, she'd pulled on the first thing she found: cropped yoga pants and an oversized sweatshirt under which she'd never bothered to put on a bra. Tony, meanwhile, was garbed in a cream-colored turtleneck sweater—cashmere, no doubt—beneath a herringbone sports coat. He probably considered the outfit casual since he'd paired it with blue jeans—the designer variety of denim that was only sold in the finest stores and cost a small fortune.

She set the box of cereal on the console table next to a jumble of magazines and unopened junk mail. As she dusted the crumbs off her hands, his gaze took in the chaos behind her.

"You'll have to excuse the mess." She wasn't strictly referring to her house.

"You have been packing, I see."

"I have a long way to go yet."

"Any progress on finding another place?"

"Since last night?" She shook her head, not sure what to make of his unexpected arrival. She decided to ask him about it. "I'm surprised to see you. In fact, I wasn't aware you knew where I lived."

"I stopped by your shop and asked the women there."

A charming smile accompanied his words. Her employees probably had tripped over one another lining up to give him Rachel's address. As gorgeous as he was, she couldn't say she blamed them. Still, she planned to have a word with them on Monday.

"And here you are," she murmured.

"I know it is rude to drop by without calling first. I hope you can forgive me."

"It's all right. I was getting ready to take a break anyway." She motioned for him to follow her and picked her way through the boxes to the couch.

"The sofa in question." He smiled as he took a seat.

"It will be sold to the highest bidder."

"So, you would rather sit on the floor." He nodded and sounded pleased.

"Yes." She cleared her throat then. "I haven't given your suggestion any more thought, if that's why you've come. I haven't had the time." She gestured to the messy room. It was a viable excuse, even if in truth she had been pondering his offer all morning. It was hard not to wonder what the future might hold when she was boxing up her old life.

"Actually, I have another idea to run by you."

Wasn't the man just full of surprises? "And what might that be?"

He glanced around the room. "I may have a temporary living arrangement for you, one that will allow you to forego moving in with family or taking your father up on his offer."

"You have my attention," she told him, and got the feeling that was exactly what he'd intended by prefacing the conversation this way.

"As you know, I'm leaving town again. I will be away for at least three months, possibly longer depending on how long it takes to wrap up my business dealings."

"And any personal dealings," Rachel inserted drily.

His brows rose. "Those, as well. I usually hire someone to look after my home while I am away. They water the plants, oversee landscaping or, as is the case this time of year, leaf and snow removal."

"What does this have to do with me?"

"You could stay there. House-sit, I believe is the term people use for such an arrangement." Tony smiled.

Rachel, meanwhile, wasn't quite sure she'd heard him right. "You want me to house-sit for you?"

"It would suit both of our needs, no?"

Something about the way he mentioned "needs" caused her flesh to prickle. Her reply was automatic. "That's a generous offer, but—"

"Generosity isn't my only motive, though I understand why you would see it that way. I need someone to look after my house. It will be sitting empty. You need a place to stay. It seems a reasonable solution to both of our problems."

"But what would you do if I wasn't in need of a place to stay?" she pressed.

"I would call a service. Hire someone I do not know."

The corners of his mouth turned down and he shrugged. "But the point is moot. You *are* in need of a place to stay, at least for the time being. This makes more sense than rushing out to rent an apartment that you may only stay in for a matter of months, does it not?"

Making sense was beyond her at the moment. But he had her interest. She asked, "And what about my belongings?"

"You said yourself you plan to sell some of your furnishings. Now you won't have to sit on the floor until you buy something to your liking. I have a very nice couch." His lips curved with a smile.

Again her flesh prickled. He seemed to have an answer for everything.

"Yet you say generosity isn't your only motive."

"Ah. You were paying attention." He smiled again. This time, she shivered. "I like you, Rachel. You intrigue me. I wouldn't mind discovering exactly why that is when I return."

Rachel's mouth fell open. She knew she should close it, but she sat their gaping at him. She half expected a television crew to pop out from another room and announce this was all a prank manufactured to entertain the masses. No one popped out, though. He was studying her, waiting patiently for a reply. She did her best to wipe the gobsmacked expression off her face.

"You would find me very boring, Tony."

"Do you think so?" he asked blandly.

Feeling self-conscious, she smoothed back wayward strands of hair and stated the obvious. "I'm not a model."

"And I am not as shallow as you apparently believe me to be. I may date models on occasion."

"As well as heiresses, actresses and debutantes," she inserted. "I've made them all jewelry, don't forget."

"A highlight of those relationships, as it turns out," he returned smoothly. "I can assure you, they are not the only sort of women I find appealing." His gaze was intense and focused on her, giving his words intimacy and impact when he added, "I find you very attractive, Rachel. I always have, but out of respect for your marriage, I never acted on it."

She ignored the unsteady *thump-thump* of her heart. "I'm flattered. Really, I am. But I'm not exactly in the market for a relationship." She exhaled on a laugh. "Which makes me rather perfect, doesn't it?"

"That sounds cynical."

"Am I wrong?" she challenged. Tony moved from one woman to the next. Bees stuck around a flower longer.

Instead of answering her question directly, he replied, "It is said that the first relationship after a divorce rarely proves long-term. Perhaps I am the one who should be concerned."

Was he mocking her? Because she couldn't be sure, she decided it was best to end the conversation. She cleared her throat. "I appreciate your interest, but—"

"But you believe it best to keep what is between us strictly professional," he finished for her.

"Yes." That certainly made the most sense. She told herself she was relieved he agreed. Whatever it was she felt, it would be short-lived.

"Perhaps you will give me the opportunity to convince you otherwise in the future." Her mouth fell open again. As she sat on the sofa trying to digest his words, Tony stood. "You still may have the use of my home. And, of course, my interest in your career has no bearing on what does or does not transpire between the two of us romantically."

"Sexually, you mean," she said bluntly.

His smile was self-assured and so sexy it made her toes want to curl. "You can have romance without sex and sex without romance, but they are better when paired together. I will leave you to decide what it is that you want, Rachel."

He started for the door.

What she wanted? She was far from certain, but one thing was clear suddenly. She was tired of making sense and toeing the line. She was tired of making compromises that left her feeling shortchanged and foolish. She'd used her head rather than following her heart when she'd married Mal. Look at where that had gotten her. She was divorced, out of a home and had barely managed to hold on to her business thanks to the settlement and the low sale price of their house.

"Tony, wait!" She pushed to her feet and met up with him in the foyer. "I appreciate your offer. Offers," she added, stressing the *s* before blurting out, "I want to take you up on them."

"All of them?"

Surprise lit his dark eyes, and no wonder. A little clarification was in order. She was neither that brave nor that impulsive. "Numbers one and two for sure. The third, we'll have to see."

"Then perhaps I should give you something to ponder while I am gone."

He drew her close as his head dipped down. His mouth was hot when it met hers. His breathing was steady, even though she couldn't seem to draw air. She felt his hand on the small of her back beneath the sweatshirt. His splayed fingers and palm were warm against her spine as they applied just enough pressure to bring her body snug against his. Her hormones began to pop and fizz like the bubbles in a celebratory glass of champagne. It wasn't just desire she felt. Even that would have been surprising. She felt desirable…and feminine…and reawakened. That sort of validation was utterly intoxicating after her long winter of discontent and self-doubt.

Their roles reversed then. It wasn't Tony she couldn't trust. It was herself. Rachel brought her hands to his chest, intending to cut the encounter short. But as the kiss deepened, her arms wound around his neck.

A moment more, just one moment more, she pleaded with her conscience.

Tony took advantage of her weakness, shifting their bodies until her back was pressed against the wall in the foyer. One of her legs was in danger of winding around his waist when the bell rang. Heidi pushed open the door even before Rachel had a chance to set both feet on the floor.

"Oh!" Heidi's eyes rounded comically as she divided her gaze between Rachel and Tony.

He recovered first.

"You must be Rachel's sister."

"And you must be every woman's fantasy," Heidi replied without missing a beat. She set a bag from a local fast-food restaurant on the console table and pulled off her gloves.

"I prefer to be called Tony."

Heidi laughed as he extended his right hand. He looked more amused than embarrassed. Meanwhile, Rachel wasn't sure how much longer she could remain upright without the support of either the foyer's wall or Tony's lean body. Her legs had turned to jelly.

"Hello, Tony. I'm Heidi. Rachel didn't mention she was going to have company."

"I stopped by unannounced."

"How lucky for her."

"He's a client," Rachel said.

Both of them glanced her way. Neither appeared convinced. Heidi, in fact, appeared to be on the verge of laughter.

"I was just leaving," Tony said.

"Don't let me chase you away."

"Actually, I have a plane to catch."

"Oh, that's too bad."

He smiled at Rachel. "I was thinking that very thing."

Despite the fact that her feet were bare, Rachel followed him out onto the porch. He dug into his pocket then and produced a key ring and a slip of paper. "These are to my house. You have the address on file. I wrote down the instructions for the front gate and the security alarm. If you need anything, I will be in New York tonight. After that, you can reach me either by cell or by calling my office in Rome."

"Tony—"

"Ciao, bella." His kissed her cheek and left.

When she stepped back inside, she was greeted by Heidi's Cheshire-cat grin.

"Don't say anything," Rachel warned.

Heidi held up her hands. "I'm not sure I know what to say. Other than *hubba-hubba*. Just where have you been hiding Mr. Tall, Dark and Sexy?"

"I haven't been hiding him anywhere."

"That's right. He's a client." Heidi winked.

"He is."

Her sister snatched the keychain out of Rachel's hand. "Oh, my God! He gave you the keys to his house."

"That's because I'm going to live there. Just until I get the renovations completed on the apartment over the shop."

Heidi's expression said she wasn't buying it. But then her skepticism transformed to concern. "I know I've been urging you to date, Rach, but maybe you need to take things a little slower. You're moving in with him?"

"He won't be there. You heard him. He's on his way to the airport. I'll be house-sitting for him. That's all."

"That's all?" Heidi crossed her arms. "You were wrapped around the man like an ivy vine."

Rachel exhaled slowly. "I know how it looked, but we're not dating. Tony is a client."

"Just a client? He's offering you the use of his home. That seems a little bit chummy to me."

Rachel ignored her. "There's nothing going on between us."

"Nothing?" Heidi prodded, brows raised.

Rachel considered the proposals Tony had made. Even if she had only agreed to the professional ones so far, there was indeed something going on between them. Heidi would want to know everything.

"Nothing."

"That's a shame." Her sister sighed. "He's so hot."

Since Rachel's pulse had yet to return to normal, she had to agree.

LATER that day, Rachel drove to Tony's house. House wasn't an apt description. She lived in a house. He lived in what would be categorized as a mansion on an estate. The massive stuccoed two-story was set back off the road. Its sizable yard was surrounded by decorative wrought-iron fencing that made it plain that trespassing was not allowed. Even though no one was home, Rachel felt underdressed for the occasion as she stopped at the gate and punched the password into the keypad. On a mechanical groan, the arms of the gate swung open in welcome.

The driveway was paved in redbrick and lined with trees that already had shed most of their leaves. As bare as their branches were, they remained stately and dignified. Rachel parked under the portico that arched from the grand front entrance, which was girded by massive white columns.

After using Tony's key, she consulted his note once again to deactivate the alarm, then she took a look around and caught her breath. Even standing in the foyer it was clear the inside was every bit as impressive as the outside had been. She slipped off her shoes and padded in her stocking feet into the living room. Tall south-facing windows flanked a fireplace that lent the large room a cozy air. She came across the dining room next. It was formal, but the eclectic assortment of art displayed both on the walls and on the sideboard made it more interesting than staid. His collection made it clear he had the eye and the wallet of a passionate collector.

Passionate. The word summed up Tony in a nutshell.

She passed through a small hallway that held a butler's pantry before entering the kitchen. Since she doubted Tony cooked, the commercial-grade stainless-steel appliances and expansive granite-topped island probably saw little use, but she could picture him sitting in the nook drinking his morning coffee, or more likely espresso, she decided, spying the maker on the countertop next to the six-burner gas stove.

A handwritten note was next to it. Rachel read it: "I have a standing account with a local market for groceries that are delivered each week. You are welcome to update the list to suit your needs. Might I suggest you keep the steak order?"

She pictured him smiling as he penned that last bit.

After a glance at the pantry, powder room and laundry, she mounted the steps to the second floor to check out the bedrooms. She came to the master first and couldn't resist opening the double doors and sneaking a peek. *Opulent* was the word that came to mind given the room's luxuriousness. It was a feast of rich colors and textures. Its walls were decorated with original art as well as some first-class reproductions. Tony definitely had an eye for beauty. Because her gaze kept straying to the king-size bed, she headed for the master bath. It turned out that the fireplace in the bedroom was double-sided. The lighting, sound system—even the window shade—were all controlled by a remote. As for the tub, it was indeed large enough to accommodate two bathers, just as he'd previously claimed. Fanning herself, she hurried out only to be confronted by that massive bed. It was way too easy to picture him lounging amid the avalanche of pillows, wearing...

Her cell phone trilled and she jumped before pulling it from her purse. It was Tony. Of course. The man seemed to have a sixth sense where she was concerned. Feeling unsettled and nosy, she backed out of the room before answering it.

"Tony, hi." Did she sound breathless? She forced a laugh. "Or should I say, *buona serra?*"

"Your accent is pretty good," he replied. "Have you had a chance to stop over at my house yet?"

"Actually, I'm here right now."

"Ah. Excellent."

"You have a lovely place, Tony."

"Thank you. What do you think of the art in my bedroom?" he asked nonchalantly.

"Wh-what do you mean?" Rachel glanced around the hallway, half expecting to spot a camera. "Why would I go in your bedroom?"

"Women are that way."

His arrogance was all the more irritating because he was right. She chose to ignore the question and asked one of her own. "Which room should I use?"

"Whichever one you prefer. And that includes the master. You'll find the bed exceptionally comfortable. I can picture you there."

"Can you?" She quashed a shiver, forced her tone to remain nonchalant. "I can't."

"Which tells me two things, *carina*."

"And they are?"

"One, you did look in my room." His laughter rumbled, the sound rich and inviting, although since it came at her expense she didn't join in.

"And the other thing?"

"If you cannot picture yourself there you need to try harder. I will talk to you soon."

With that he hung up, which was just as well. The last thing Rachel needed to be doing right now was picturing either of them, much less both of them, in that decadent-looking king-size bed.

LATE that evening, Tony settled on the couch in his Manhattan apartment with a glass of wine. His flight from Detroit's Metropolitan Airport to LaGuardia had been delayed by a couple of hours, giving him plenty of time to think. Too much time, perhaps.

Rachel was moving into his house.

He knew better than to think that she would sleep in his bed. He sipped his merlot. That would take time and finesse on his part. The three months he expected to be away would give him the perfect opportunity to romance her. He believed in romance. It was a dance of sorts, a means to an end. Pretty words, sparkly trinkets, stolen kisses and fleeting caresses—they not only ensured the end result, in Tony's experience, they made it all the more enjoyable.

Besides, Rachel deserved romance.

He frowned and pushed to his feet, then paced to the French doors that opened to a balcony that, during the day, offered a stunning panoramic view of Central Park. Even though it was chilly, he went out and stood at the railing, immune to the sounds of traffic from the street below.

He'd never met a woman more unaware of her innate attractiveness or more uncertain of her femininity. Repressed. He kept coming back to that word. It wasn't that Tony only considered Rachel a challenge, though definitely she would be one. He wasn't the sort of man who looked at women as conquests. He wasn't that cold. He may have bruised a few hearts over the years, but he'd never intentionally set out to break any. That was why he ended his relationships before they could become too involved and messy. The most recent one with Astrid was a case in point. When she'd requested a key to his hotel suite in Stockholm, he'd known it was time to move on. He refused to consider how easily he'd handed over the key to his home to Rachel. But, then, Rachel hadn't asked for it and had been hesitant to take it. He'd had to talk her into it, arguing the benefits of the arrangement. Indeed, she was a challenge on so many levels.

Tony finished off his wine and went back inside. In the kitchen, he poured himself a second glass and thought of the pendant necklace Rachel had created for Astrid. He'd meant it when he'd told her he could take her places. He knew exactly the sort of people she needed to meet. People with pockets every bit as deep as his own who would be willing not only to purchase her wares but bankroll an expanded business venture. He could do it himself, but he wasn't sure that was the best idea since he wanted to sleep with her, too.

The phone rang as he made a mental list. Glancing at the caller ID, he sighed before answering. It was his mother.

"Buona serra, Mama."

She didn't bother with pleasantries, she launched into a lecture. "You said you would call to let me know you arrived home safely."

"Mama, I am thirty-eight years old," he reminded her.

"And I am your mother. I worry, Tony. I worry the same now as I did when you were a chubby-cheeked toddler. Have babies of your own and you will understand."

He sidestepped what he knew would turn into a diatribe on his lifestyle and single status. "I am home safe. Just having some warm milk before I turn in for the night."

"It is a sin to lie to your mother. You are having wine." Lucia's laughter rumbled a moment, but then she grew serious. "I do worry about you, Tony. Thursday is Thanksgiving and you will be spending it alone. You need a wife, someone you love. You need a reason to want to stay home more."

It was an old conversation, but tonight it left him feeling unsettled. He blamed fatigue for the fact that the portrait of domestic bliss his mother painted with her words was juxtaposed against his attraction for a woman who soon would be setting up housekeeping in his home.

CHAPTER SIX

RACHEL sat across the table from her ex-husband in a conference room at the real-estate office. Mal's girlfriend was seated next to him, her chair pulled snug against his. Any closer and Alyssa would have been in his lap. In addition to looking as if she could be cutting high-school math class to be there, her expression was annoyingly smug. And no wonder. She'd gotten everything. Rachel's husband and now Rachel's house.

Well, she was welcome to both. Still, it rankled. Rachel felt duped. Again.

"You could have mentioned that Alyssa was the buyer," she said through gritted teeth. For that matter, their agent should have piped up about it during that first phone conversation. But Flora hadn't breathed a word.

"I didn't see the relevance," Mal replied in the same bored tone he'd used so often during the last year of their marriage.

Next to him, Alyssa smacked her gum and smiled.

Looking at him now, Rachel wondered why she'd tried so hard to save her marriage. Had it always been this obvious, how little the two of them had in common? How little they understood one another? Had she loved him or had she loved the idea of being married to someone the polar opposite of her irresponsible father? She *had* played it safe.

She'd been a fool in more ways than one. She couldn't blame Mal for that. But she could blame him for this.

"You didn't see the relevance?"

Despite her best efforts, her voice rose. Mal glanced uncomfortably toward the open door. They were waiting for their agent to return with the necessary paperwork to finalize the sale. Alyssa didn't have an agent. She'd used Flora to represent her in the sale. Conflict of interest was written all over the situation, as far as Rachel was concerned.

"I wouldn't have agreed to drop the price by ten grand, throw in the kitchen appliances and pay all of the closing costs had I realized that you would be moving back in and setting up housekeeping with your teenage paramour."

"Hey, let's get one thing straight. I'm not a teenager," Alyssa piped in. "I don't know what a paramour is, but Mal and I are engaged now."

The young woman waggled the fingers on her left hand. The diamond, a brilliant-cut full carat set in platinum, sparkled festively under the florescent lights. Even without her jeweler's loupe, Rachel could tell its quality probably didn't match its price tag. Still, it made a nice complement to the oversized diamond earrings whose receipt Rachel had discovered, setting off the chain of events that found them here.

Mal had the grace to flush. "I was going to tell you."

"Why? We're divorced. But you'll understand if I don't offer my congratulations," Rachel added drily.

"You had to know it was coming."

"Just like I should have known you were cheating on me?"

Across the table, Mal flushed again, but this time Rachel saw temper flare in his eyes.

"You were always so damned busy with your shop. You weren't content just to own the place. No. You had to start designing jewelry. It got to be that was all you cared about."

The accusation wasn't new. It still made her uncomfortable, in part because she knew he was right.

"I'm sorry, Mal."

"What?"

"I'm sorry. You're right. I wasn't being fair to you." Even if she wasn't the only one who'd worked sixty-hour weeks. She didn't add that she hadn't been fair to herself, either.

Mal blinked, taken aback by her words and the conciliatory tone in which they were offered.

"Do you mean that?" he asked.

Tony's face came to mind. He was smiling. Of course.

"You know what? I do. I really do."

Mal relaxed. Was he feeling a weight lifted? Perhaps a little guilt seep away? Whatever. She could be magnanimous...on that score. The house was another matter. She told him as much.

"I think we both know that, given what has just now come to light, if I wanted to raise a stink over the sale, I could. In fact, if I wanted to be difficult, I could walk out of here right now without signing the papers and call my lawyer. What the three of you hatched is unethical, if not outright illegal. Don't think for a minute that I see this as fulfilling the terms of our divorce settlement."

Mal's eyes narrowed. "Are you trying to wiggle out of paying me back for the loan to your business?"

"Not at all." She wouldn't leave here today beholden to him. "I'll repay you every cent I owe. That's only fair. And fairness is what I expect from you in return. In fact, I'm demanding it. Or I walk out right now."

She'd so rarely made waves during their marriage that her uncompromising tone probably came as a shock.

Across from her, Mal looked a little sick. Alyssa fingered her gaudy engagement ring and worked her gum.

Their agent returned as the silence lengthened. Flora glanced around the table, no doubt taking in their tight expressions. She forced a bright smile to her lips.

"All righty then," she said uneasily. She tapped the bottom edges of the papers on the table. "I think I have everything in order."

"There's been a change in the terms," Rachel announced and had the satisfaction of hearing Mal swear as he wilted back in his seat. "It turns out I will be keeping the appliances, Flora, and Alyssa has generously agreed to pay the closing costs as well as both portions of your commission."

When Mal opened his mouth to protest, Rachel said, "Be glad I'm not pushing for full asking price and the use of the place until the apartment is ready. As it happens I've already made other living arrangements."

A muscle ticked in Mal's jaw before he nodded.

"But, honey," Alyssa began.

He ignored her and turned his attention to their wide-eyed and ashen agent. "Write it up, Flora."

Flora looked eager to comply, if only because it took her out of the conference room. When she returned with a fresh batch of papers a little later, Rachel happily scrawled her signature on this dotted line and that, supplied the date and her initials where necessary. Twenty minutes later, she walked out of the office into the late afternoon's waning light with a huge grin on her face.

A long, unpleasant chapter in her life was officially closed. It was time to start another, one she would write herself.

Designing jewelry is all you care about.

She mulled Mal's accusation as she got in her car and

revved its engine to life. This time, instead of guilt or annoyance, it was validation she felt. Oh, she cared about more than designing jewelry, but now it could and would be her focus without any guilt or regrets.

Rachel was in the mood to celebrate. The image of Tony Salerno outfitted in a tuxedo sprang to mind. If anyone knew how to mark a momentous occasion, he would. At least, that's what she told herself in order to corral the butterflies that took flight in her stomach whenever he entered her thoughts these days.

She waited until she stopped for a light before pulling out her cell phone and dialing the shop to let her assistant know she wouldn't be returning after all.

"Is everything all right, Mrs. Palmer?" Jenny asked.

The young woman's concern was touching and understandable; Rachel never missed work.

"I'm better than all right, Jenny. And call me Ms. Preston now," she added, supplying her maiden name.

She would be calling her lawyer after all. How much trouble would it be to legally change her name? Certainly no more hassle than going through a divorce, dividing up assets and hiring a contractor to convert commercial storage space into a studio apartment, Rachel decided as she started in the direction of Tony's house—her house for the time being. She'd been there to supervise the unloading of most of her belongings earlier that day. The rest had gone to storage, either at the small unit she'd rented or the shop for smaller items. She would be sending the movers back for her appliances first thing in the morning. For now, she was going to bask in her triumph.

A smile spread slowly across her face. She planned to make good use of the many high-end amenities at her disposal, in particular the big and decidedly decadent jetted tub she'd spied in the master bathroom. It had all of the most modern bells and whistles, including an underwater sound system. She wouldn't need to light candles, either. She would light the fire.

Ah, yes. Decadent indeed.

On the way, she stopped to pick up a bottle of champagne. She wasn't a fan of bubbly or alcohol in general. She drank only occasionally and then in small amounts since alcohol caused her cheeks to turn an unbecoming and uncomfortably warm shade of red. But the occasion called for it, even if she only indulged in a sip.

"Maybe I'll bathe in it," she murmured aloud.

She had unpacking to do. Plenty of it. Still, when she arrived at the house, Rachel didn't dive into the chore that greeted her in her suite. Just inside the threshold, she kicked off her shoes and began stripping off her clothes— a boring cream sweater and equally unimaginative black pants whose fit had never been flattering. She left them in a heap on the floor, deciding on the spot that she would never wear either again. She might even burn them. She wanted color, pizzazz. That new chapter was already being written.

She didn't miss the symbolism. She was indeed undergoing a transformation, a metamorphosis from duped and dumped wife to empowered woman. Make that savvy businesswoman. She retrieved her cell from the pocket of her discarded pants and, champagne bottle in hand, she entered Tony's inner sanctum.

As she sat on the edge of the tub, waiting for it to fill, she dialed the contact number Tony had given her. He sounded groggy when he answered, and no wonder.

"I forgot about the time difference. Sorry."

"Rachel?"

"Yes. Sorry," she said again. Her enthusiasm of a moment ago began to ebb. "I'll hang up now."

"No. Wait!"

She heard the rustling of fabric and imagined Tony freeing himself from a tangle of sheets. From the legs of a slumbering woman, as well? Rachel closed her eyes, but the vivid image remained.

"I'll call back." She hung up without waiting for his response.

The tub was full. She slipped into the water and let out a long sigh. She was trying to figure out how to start the jets and cue the music when her cell rang. She knew exactly who was on the other end of the line.

"You didn't have to call me back," she said without preamble. "I didn't mean to bother you."

"You are never a bother, Rachel." He sounded sincere. "Is everything all right?"

"It is. Better than all right, in fact. That's why I called, I guess. I'm looking to the future."

"Any reason in particular?"

"I closed on the house today."

"You sound happy."

"I am. I did a little renegotiating." She filled him in on what had transpired in the agent's office.

"You let them off easy," Tony said.

"Probably. I was feeling sentimental. It turns out they are engaged." Although it hadn't been funny at the time, Rachel started to laugh. "The next Mrs. Palmer waved her engagement ring in my face."

"No doubt its quality is as second-rate as she is."

Rachel grinned. "You're very good for my ego."

"Am I now?" He sounded pleased. His tone lifted several notches on the sexy scale when he added, "I could be very good for you in other ways."

Rachel ignored the flutter in her belly and changed the subject. "Alyssa wasn't sure what a paramour was."

"Alyssa?"

"The next Mrs. Palmer. Very busty, but not too bright."

"Some men are intimidated by intelligent women, since they are not as easy to manipulate. It sounds like Mal should have married her the first time around."

"It certainly would have saved us both a lot of headaches."

"And heartache?"

"That, too." She could have left it at that, and probably should have, but she heard herself add, "I realized something today. I was as much to blame as Mal. Well, maybe not quite as much. I didn't break any vows. But I shouldn't have made any in the first place."

"You were playing it safe," he replied smugly.

They'd had this conversation already. "No one likes to hear, 'I told you so.'"

"Perdonilo." Then Tony said, "Since Mal will be moving back into the house, did you offer to sell him the beige couch?"

Rachel burst out laughing. Oh, yes. Tony was definitely good for her ego.

"No. I'm selling it and a lot of other stuff online. When the apartment over the shop is finally ready, I plan to buy something red with modern lines."

"Excellent. Speaking of the move, are you all settled in at my house?"

"More or less. I still have unpacking to do. In fact, I should be doing it now, but I'm relaxing."

"You are not at work?" His surprise was plain.

Rachel wiggled her toes under the water. She could do with a pedicure. Maybe she'd schedule one for tomorrow. "I'm playing hooky for the rest of the day and seriously thinking about making an appointment for some spa pampering in the morning."

Deep laughter rumbled from the other end of the line. She pictured the corners of Tony's eyes crinkling with amusement when he teased, "So, you *were* paying attention when I spoke about making time to play."

"I guess I was. I've become too dull. It's time to break out of my shell."

"I would like to be there to see that."

She shifted her position in the tub, causing the water to slosh.

Tony homed in on it like a hound dog on the hunt. "Where exactly are you right now?"

Rachel sank a little lower in the water. It was time to come clean in more ways than one. "I'm in your tub."

"You are in my tub?" His tone was low and oddly intense.

"I should have asked first. I—"

"*Madonna mia!* I guess I no longer have to wonder what you are wearing."

That drew out a smile. Still, she added, "I hope you're not upset."

"I am. With myself that I am on a different continent when I could be there with you."

The words sounded sincere. Indeed, spoken in his sleep-roughened Italian accent, they sounded way too sexy. It didn't help that she was naked. Rachel felt that flutter in her belly again.

"Regardless of which continent you're on, I'm sure you're not lacking for female companionship."

He was quiet a moment. She took his silence for agreement. When he did speak, he asked, "Did you light the fire?"

She glanced to where flames frolicked in hues of orange and yellow behind the glass insert. "I did."

"And music? I do not hear anything playing in the background."

"I haven't figured out the remote yet," she admitted. "It looks like it's big enough to launch a rocketship."

"Shall I help you?"

The offer warmed her skin even more than the heated bathwater.

"I'd appreciate that. Thanks."

"Excellent. The right music and lighting will enhance the experience," he assured her.

He explained how to operate the remote, walking her through the steps. In short order, the lights were dimmed and Andrea Bocelli's silken tenor was echoing softly off the Carrara marble.

Even though Rachel was starting to feel stirred up, she told Tony, "You certainly know how to relax."

"Anything worth doing is worth doing well."

From his tone it was clear he wasn't speaking only of relaxing.

"Bragging?" she challenged.

"It's only bragging if you are not able to back it up, *carina*. Would you care to test me?"

An ocean's worth of separation made her brave. Instead of telling him no, she replied, "As you said, you're on another continent."

She thought she heard him mutter *"Madonna mia"* again before he asked, "And if I were not?"

"I guess we'll never know."

"Oh, we will," he assured her. "Another time, we will. You are not ready yet."

Rachel wanted to be turned off by his arrogant certainty. Instead, her body hummed and need began to churn.

"No response?"

She glanced down to where the peaks of her breasts crested the water. "I wouldn't say that."

"I need a glass of wine," he mumbled. He didn't sound quite so cocky now. "Have you poured yourself one?"

"Actually, I have champagne." She concentrated on the uncorked bottle. Her gaze followed the progress of a bead of condensation. It started slow at the neck, picking up momentum until it reached the base. It made her think of sex. Of course, at the moment, everything had her thinking about sex.

"You are full of surprises."

"I'm not drinking it. In fact, I haven't even opened the bottle."

"Do you need me to walk you through that process, as well?" Tony asked.

"I haven't decided whether I want to drink it or not. I don't really like champagne."

"You don't like champagne? Why did you buy it?"

"I was in the mood to celebrate."

"Ah, yes. Your liberation," he said.

It was an interesting take on divorce. One she wouldn't have agreed with mere weeks ago. But it was on the mark, Rachel realized now. She hadn't been set free from marriage to Mal as much as set free from her own limited expectations when it came to her life and her heart. Still, that wasn't the only reason she'd bought the bubbly.

"I've been doing a lot of thinking about my future as it pertains to jewelry design. I have so many ideas that I've put off even considering because, well, I felt limited."

"No limits now. And no strings. I want you, *carina*. Make no mistake about that. But I meant it when I said that one thing has nothing to do with the other. Our personal and professional relationships will remain independent of one another. Now, let me get a glass of wine and I will join you in a toast."

"I'd better not have any champagne. I have an adverse reaction to alcohol."

"A lot of people do." Humor leaked into his tone. "Unfortunately, that doesn't stop them from overindulging."

"In my case, a couple of sips and I get all hot."

"I can only imagine," he replied. In addition to humor-filled, his voice now sounded strained. "So what will you do with the champagne if you do not drink it?"

"I don't know. I may add it to the bath water," she remarked recklessly.

"You are enjoying torturing me," he accused on a chuckle.

She laughed, as well. "Maybe I am, just a little."

"How is the water?"

"Warm. And it feels wonderful. You're torturing yourself now, Tony."

"Apparently you bring out masochistic tendencies I was unaware I had." Then, "About that champagne, I want you to open it right now. Indulge me, yes?"

"Sorry. I didn't think to bring a glass."

"Do you need one?"

"You want me to drink it from the bottle?"

"That is not what I meant. I thought you were going to bathe in it. I like that idea. And I am curious how it would feel to have those bubbles on your skin. You can describe it to me. In detail."

"You're incorrigible," she said as her heart rapped out an unsteady rhythm.

At the moment, so was she. It hadn't slipped her notice that they were engaging in what qualified as foreplay, albeit by telephone. Still, Rachel would see him in the flesh again at some point. She needed to remember that and take care not to send signals she had no intention of making good on, lest their next meeting be awkward.

She liked Tony, and their attraction was definitely mutual, but she needed to tread with care. It wasn't only that he was a valued client of Expressive Gems. Now that she had accepted his offer to help her expand her jewelry-design business they were entering a partnership of sorts. He might claim one had no bearing on the other, but…

"I think I'd better hang up now."

"That is probably a good idea," he said slowly, seriously.

"Good night, Tony."

"Buona notte."

Tony hung up, but he knew better than to think he would fall back to sleep. Not now. He pushed a hand through his hair and groaned. He was picturing Rachel in his bath, picturing himself slipping into the heated water beside her. Their hips bumping. Legs twining. Bare skin sliding over bare skin. He closed his eyes and swore under his breath when the image not only remained but became more vivid.

The fantasy was one of many Tony had had of Rachel recently. The woman had definitely gotten under his skin, and Tony was left with the uneasy and unprecedented feeling that he might be in over his head.

CHAPTER SEVEN

BARELY an hour later, Tony's phone rang again. He smiled as he reached for it, expecting—or at least hoping—that Rachel would be on the other end.

His mother's agitated voice greeted him instead.

"There is a woman in your home!"

Lucia rattled off half a dozen more words in Italian, making it plain what she thought of a member of the opposite sex setting up housekeeping under her only son's roof, especially a woman she had never met.

He swung his feet over the side of the mattress and sat up. This wasn't the sort of call one took lying down.

"Mama, Mama. Calm yourself. It is not what you are thinking," he began.

"Are you telling me that you are not involved with this woman? She is in your home, Tony. Right now. Along with boxes and boxes of her belongings! You are living with a woman!"

Even though he couldn't see Lucia, Tony knew his mother was gesturing wildly with her arms. Under other circumstances, he might have chuckled, but Lucia wasn't in the mood to find humor in this.

"Her name is Rachel Palmer—"

"She introduced herself as Rachel Preston. Preston, Tony. Not Palmer. *Non ci porro credere!* You don't even know her name! You are living with a woman and you don't even know her name!"

"I know her name." Although the Preston bit came as a surprise. Maiden name, most likely, and she was opting to go back to it, which was what he told his mother now. That proved the verbal equivalent of throwing kerosene on a roaring bonfire.

"She is divorced?" His mother's voice rose several octaves on the two-syllable word.

"She is. It is not a crime, Mama. One in two marriages end in divorce."

"Not when you take your vows seriously," Lucia replied. "Is she Catholic?"

Uh-oh. Talk of vows, whether taken or untaken, was not a direction he wanted to go, especially when religion was being thrown into the mix.

"I have no idea."

"You donna know?"

"Her faith has never come up in our conversations, which have centered primarily on *business*," Tony stressed.

As soon as he said it, guilt nipped, since lately that wasn't true. Indeed, if his mother were privy to his earlier conversation with Rachel, she would be chastising him for lying.

As it was, Lucia uttered a quick prayer to the Blessed Mother and then wailed, "Oh, Tony! If she is Catholic, you are living in sin with a divorced woman. You may as well be committing adultery. It is the same thing."

He pictured Lucia crossing herself. In the eyes of his devout mother, Rachel's marriage would only be considered null and void if she sought and was granted an annulment through the Church.

"Mama, I am not living with Rachel," he began patiently. "I am in Rome. Rachel is staying at my house. You

Send For
2 FREE BOOKS
Today!

I accept your offer!

Please send me two
free Harlequin® Romance
novels and two mystery
gifts (gifts worth about $10).
I understand that these books
are completely free—even
the shipping and handling will
be paid—and I am under no
obligation to purchase anything, ever,
as explained on the back of this card.

❏ I prefer the regular-print edition
116/316 HDL FMST

❏ I prefer the larger-print edition
186/386 HDL FMST

Please Print

FIRST NAME

LAST NAME

ADDRESS

APT.#   CITY

STATE/PROV.   ZIP/POSTAL CODE

Visit us online at
www.ReaderService.com

NO POSTAGE
NECESSARY
IF MAILED
IN THE
UNITED STATES

BUSINESS REPLY MAIL
FIRST-CLASS MAIL   PERMIT NO. 717   BUFFALO, NY

POSTAGE WILL BE PAID BY ADDRESSEE

THE READER SERVICE

PO BOX 1867

BUFFALO NY 14240-9952

will notice that those *boxes and boxes* of belongings are in the guest room. That is because she is a guest."

Guilt nipped again, this time with a little more bite. But at least his mother sounded slightly mollified. Her tone was no longer shrill when she said, "I did notice that the boxes were in the guest room."

"So you understand?" He began to relax. He should have known better.

"I am not a fool, Tony. The boxes may be in the guest room, but *she* is in your bathtub! Or at least she was when I walked in there. And she was naked!" Lucia added unnecessarily.

The mental image Tony had done his damnedest to forget for the past hour was back in full living color. Tony caught himself before he could groan.

"Should she have been wearing a swimsuit?"

"You no get smart with me, Antonio Rafael." He might be a grown man, but his mother wasn't one to tolerate back talk regardless of his age, as her use of his middle name clearly showed.

"I am sorry, Mama. I only mean to point out that one usually takes a bath without clothing."

"But if she is a guest, why is she in the tub in your suite? Hmm? Tell me that."

"Because it is nicer. And larger. And it has a fireplace and music," he said.

"You have answers for everything," Lucia muttered. "Same as when you were a little boy. You have always been good at talking yourself out of trouble."

His mother sighed then, a signal that she'd given up. At least for now. He knew better than to believe she wouldn't revisit this topic. Several more times. She could be as tenacious as a pit bull.

"Where is Rachel now?"

"How am I to know? I left her alone."

"But you are still at my house."

"I am. Downstairs. I am in your neglected kitchen putting your fancy stove to use. I am making marinara. You have several fat tomatoes that are ready to go bad. And I have pulled out your pasta machine. I had to wipe off a thick layer of dust, but I think it still works."

Even though he wished she had gone home to her own kitchen to do it, Tony couldn't help smiling. His mother cooked whenever she was upset or worried or experiencing any one of a dozen other emotions. After his father died, Lucia had made enough fresh pasta and her signature marinara to feed all of Florence. For a week. Though he'd only been a young boy at the time, he remembered too well her sadness and the helplessness he'd felt when he could offer no real comfort, in part because he was grieving himself.

Everyone kept saying, "You are the man of the house now, Antonio."

Men fixed things. But his mother's heart, much like their lives, had seemed beyond repair. Then Paolo Russo came along. Tony respected his stepfather. But it was because Paolo had made Lucia smile again that Tony had been willing to accept him into their lives and hand over the reins.

"She is too skinny."

His mother's muttered words pulled him from his thoughts. Tony agreed with her assessment. Rachel had always been slender, but she was even thinner now, most likely the result of all of the emotional upheaval she'd endured. But he knew in addition to trying to fatten up Rachel, his mother was going to grill her. Mercilessly. Before Lucia was done, Rachel would feel more exposed than she must have felt when his mother interrupted her bath. He needed to try to talk his mother out of it.

He cleared his throat, a sound she apparently took as agreement, because she continued, "All of the women you date are too skinny. At least from the pictures I have seen. Pictures, Antonio. I never get to meet any of them. Not since Kendra."

And he had worried about Rachel. He was still in the hot seat.

"You know why that is, Mama," he said softly.

His mother had become very attached to the woman he'd almost married. In the end, Tony's heart hadn't been the only casualty. He'd never made that mistake again, no matter how much Lucia or his sister pestered him.

Lucia muttered something he couldn't quite make out, which he figured was for the best. It probably wasn't anything he wanted to hear anyway.

"Don't stay too long, Mama. And, please, don't make a habit of dropping in unannounced. Rachel is using my home now and is entitled to her privacy. What were you doing at my house anyway?" he asked. To lighten the mood, he added, "Were you thinking of putting my tub to good use?"

Lucia made a dismissive sound. "I came to clean out your refrigerator. That is how I knew about the perfectly good tomatoes that would soon go to waste."

"I have people I can pay to clean out my refrigerator for me."

"Yes." Her seeming agreement didn't last long. "You also have a mother who considers it no trouble at all."

And who probably saw it as a good opportunity to get in a little snooping.

"So, what are you making?" Tony figured he could

judge the length of Lucia's stay based on what she was planning to put in the oven.

"Lasagna. I am preparing the tomatoes for the sauce as we speak."

And she'd said the pasta would be made from scratch, too. Tony stifled a groan. His mother was going to be there for hours.

RACHEL paced around the boxes in her room, debating what to do next. She wasn't sure who the woman was who had burst into the bathroom. They hadn't exactly had a chance to exchange greetings. Rachel had screamed and, in her attempt to cover herself, had knocked the bottle of champagne off the ledge of the tub. No need to worry about popping the cork. The bottle had shattered. Champagne had splattered. After demanding to know Rachel's identity, the older woman had shouted something in what sounded like Italian, and stormed out.

Was she still in the house?

Rachel didn't know. She'd gotten out of the tub, carefully picked her way through the worst of the glass and spilled sparkling wine, and now was in her room, dressed in the same boring clothes she'd vowed to burn, pacing the floor and wondering what she should do next.

If the woman still was downstairs, and if she was a relative of Tony's—please, God, don't let it be his mother—she was entitled to an explanation, not to mention an introduction that consisted of more than a bloodcurdling scream and a shouted name. Besides, Rachel needed to clean up the mess she'd made in the bathroom.

She followed the sounds of clanking pans and soaring opera music to the kitchen. Swallowing the worst of her nerves, she entered. The older woman stood at the island. A dish towel was tucked around her waist and she'd pushed up the sleeves of her blouse to her elbows. She was rolling out dough on the flour-dusted granite top. She looked up and stopped what she was doing when she saw Rachel. She didn't smile, exactly. In fact, she looked quite formidable. It didn't help that she was wielding a fat wooden rolling pin.

"Hello. I'm a friend of Tony's."

"Yes, I know. I called my son." Son. Uh-oh. "Rachel Preston, as you said. Or Rachel Palmer, according to Tony."

"It's Palmer for now, but I will be changing it back to Preston. Tony was kind enough to let me stay here until the renovation work on my new place is done."

"You are a house guest." The older woman nodded. "He told me that, too."

"Oh." Not sure what else to say, Rachel fell silent.

"If you are looking for a mop, I think you will find it in the storage closet in the laundry room."

"Mop. Right. Thank you."

The older woman's expression softened a little. "I should apologize for barging in on you. I wasn't expecting anyone to be home. I heard the music and I thought that Tony might have left it on by accident."

"It's all right."

"We have not been properly introduced. I am Lucia Russo."

"It's nice to meet you, Mrs. Russo."

"Lucia, please. There is no need for such formality between us."

"Lucia," Rachel repeated.

"And I don't believe you, by the way."

"Excuse me?"

The corners of a mouth very much like Tony's turned

up in a smile. "I do not think that *you think* it is so nice to meet me. I gave you quite a start earlier."

"A little," Rachel admitted. She took a step closer to the island. "What is it that you're making?"

"Lasagna." She started to work again with the rolling pin.

Rachel's gaze strayed to the stove top where something was already simmering in a pan, to a chopping block where cloves of garlic and onion had already been minced and chopped, and then back to Lucia. "From scratch?"

"Is there any other way?" The older woman's challenge was issued with another smile.

"I've never made pasta from scratch, let alone an entire pan of lasagna." She decided it best not to admit the only lasagna she'd ever eaten at home had come premade and frozen.

"It is not so hard once you learn," Lucia replied as she rolled out more dough. "Come back when you have cleaned up the broken glass. I will show you how."

Rachel did as she was told. Tony's mother did not look like the kind of woman who took no for an answer, but that wasn't the only reason she returned downstairs twenty minutes later. She was curious—about Lucia and Tony and, yes, how to make lasagna. Rachel was a decent cook, though much of what she knew she'd learned on her own. Susan Preston hadn't had either the time or the energy to cook from scratch while raising two girls alone.

"Put this around your waist as an apron," Lucia said, handing Rachel a dishcloth as soon as she entered the kitchen. "So skinny," she muttered while Rachel did as instructed.

Then it began: Rachel's tutorial in Italian cooking. Lucia moved with both grace and efficiency between the island and the stove. In a large pot on the front burner, chopped onions were starting to caramelize in olive oil. The tomatoes, which had been peeled and seeded, sat in a glass bowl near to the stove. An assortment of spice jars were next to it.

"I will teach you how to make a good marinara. This was my mother's recipe, handed down to her from her mother. It is a basic sauce that can be fancied up with other ingredients as one sees fit." Lucia smiled. "It is what you might call the little black dress of sauces."

She made more small talk as she showed Rachel the proper way to skin and mince cloves of garlic. Once they were added to the pot with the onion, Lucia began opening jars of dried spices and the inquest began.

Lucia was subtle at first. As she shook some oregano into the palm of her hand, she said, "Tony tells me you are waiting for an apartment to become ready."

"Yes. It's over the jewelry store I own downtown. Unfortunately, my house sold before the renovations were complete."

Lucia tossed the oregano in the pot and shook out a similar amount of sweet basil into her hand. "The house where you lived while married?"

"Yes."

Lucia hummed, tossed in the basil and picked up the thyme. "What is the name of the church where you were married?"

"Actually, we got married at City Hall."

"Not very romantic," Lucia commented, but she looked relieved as she measured out dried rosemary.

"No, it wasn't all that romantic, but it seemed practical at the time." Eager to change the subject, Rachel motioned to the spice jars. "How do you know how much to add of each one?"

"After so many years, I just know." Lucia pursed her

lips in consideration. "I guess for a batch of sauce this size I would figure on about two tablespoons in total. I add more basil than rosemary, but that is my preference. You will have to decide for yourself."

Even before Rachel had a chance to make a mental note of that, Lucia was saying, "But now you want romance."

"I—" Was that Tony's appeal? The more she got to know him, the less she thought so. "I'm not sure what I want," Rachel answered honestly.

Lucia nodded and seemed satisfied. "If you use fresh herbs, you would not add them yet. You would need to wait until just before serving. They would lose too much of their flavor otherwise."

"Dried herbs early, fresh ones later."

The smells emanating from the pot had Rachel's mouth threatening to water. It went dry just as fast when, without warning, Lucia asked, "Do you think my son is handsome?"

"T-Tony?"

Lucia tapped the spatula against the inside of the pot to free it of bits of onion. "I only have one son."

How to answer that question except with the truth? "Too handsome."

Lucia's robust laughter filled the kitchen. "His father was the same way. Tony takes after him, not only in appearance but in here." Lucia patted her ample bosom. "He is a good man."

"I agree."

Lucia reached for an opened bottle of red wine. After adding some to the pot, she filled a glass for herself.

"Would you like some?"

"No, thank you."

"Tony also is generous," Lucia remarked.

"Exceptionally so when it comes to women." Rachel

felt heat creep up her neck to her cheeks. What a thing to say! Especially since she was staying rent-free at his home. She backtracked. "What I mean is, I've designed jewelry for so many of his girlfriends."

Oh, that was *much* better. Rachel grimaced and clamped her lips closed. Good heavens! Every time she opened her mouth and spoke, she wound up digging herself a deeper hole. She might as well have called him a jet-setting playboy right to his mother's face. It was a description that not all that long ago Rachel would have thought fit. Now...

Lucia, however, didn't look the least bit offended. Indeed, the older woman sighed heavily and stirred the contents of the pot again.

"Now it is time to add the tomatoes I skinned and chopped earlier."

"It already smells wonderful."

"It is far from finished. Patience is required in cooking, and in many other things, to achieve the desired result." She sent Rachel a meaningful look. "This sauce will need to simmer for a couple of hours in order to bring out the flavor of the spices."

"That long, hmm?" Which meant the inquest would continue.

"Do not worry. We have plenty to do. In the meantime, you and I will finish making the pasta."

They were back at the granite-topped island. Lucia patted an odd-looking appliance. It appeared brand-new. Its stainless-steel finish gleamed and showed nary a fingerprint.

Lucia's tone made it clear she was not impressed.

"This is Tony's fancy pasta maker. It has a motor. I prefer the old-fashioned one I have owned for nearly forty years. I crank it myself. No need for electricity. And I think the pasta tastes just as good if not better." She shrugged. "But we will make do with this one."

As Rachel helped to feed the thinly rolled dough into the machine, Lucia continued talking.

"This is a nice kitchen, no?"

"Yes. Very."

"Tony rarely eats in here. And why would he? He is a bachelor. I only hope I will live long enough to see my son settled down with the right woman." In the same breath, Lucia added, "So, your marriage, it did not work out."

Rachel nearly dropped the thinly rolled dough she was feeding into the pasta machine. "No."

"Your divorce, it was recent?"

"It was final last month." She heard herself add, "But it was over long before then."

"No children?"

"No."

"You do not want children?"

Caught in the crosshairs, Rachel sputtered, "I…um, sure. That is, someday."

"You are not getting any younger."

"So my mother tells me."

"That is because she wants grandchildren," Lucia said on a nod. "You hope to marry again, then?"

"I haven't given the idea much thought," Rachel replied honestly. Even so, she knew immediately that it was not the right answer.

"Yet you already know you want children. Will you be having those without the benefit of a wedding ring and the support of a husband?"

"Oh. I—"

"Have not given it much thought?" Lucia did not look convinced.

Rachel thought she knew why. She decided to reassure the older woman that she had no designs on her son.

"I've decided it's best to concentrate on my career right now. You know, Tony has been a valued client of mine over the years, and he believes I can expand my design business. He's agreed to help me in that regard."

"So, your relationship with Tony is business."

"Yes. That's all."

"That is *all?*" Lucia turned Rachel's statement into a question.

"Well, we are friends, too, which I guess is obvious since I'm staying here while my apartment is being renovated and he is away."

"Ah, yes. Friends." Lucia nodded. "You are special, then."

"Excuse me?"

"You are the only friend of Tony's that I know who is a woman."

"Really? I had no idea."

Rachel was left with the distinct impression Lucia didn't believe her. But somehow she must have managed to pass maternal muster because three hours later, when the older woman pulled on her coat to leave, she said to Rachel, "You will come to my home for Thanksgiving if you have no other plans. Tony will not be there, unfortunately. But you come."

"Thank you for the invitation. I'm having dinner with my mom and sister."

Lucia was not the sort of woman who took no for an answer, however.

"Just for dessert, then. I will give you my recipe for tiramisu. It is Tony's favorite. As his *friend* I think you should learn how to make it."

CHAPTER EIGHT

THREE weeks passed. They dragged by, actually. Tony was going to be away for far longer before this trip was done. But for the first time in years, he felt restless to return to the States—Michigan in particular, since his family was there. It was approaching the holidays, he told himself. They made him nostalgic, which was why he'd already made plans to fly in for Christmas, stay for the day, and then fly back out. He had a meeting in New York the following day. New Year's Eve would find him in Rome at the annual party of a business colleague and friend.

His mother would never forgive him if he missed a second big family dinner. As it was, he had yet to hear the end of it for being absent on Thanksgiving Day.

Rachel had been there, not for the actual meal but for dessert. She'd dropped by at his mother's invitation—command was more like it. Lucia was hard to say no to. She had told Tony all about Rachel's visit during a phone call later that same night, waking him up a full two hours before his alarm was set to go off. His sister, meanwhile, had sent a detailed email the following day.

"She's nice. I like her, Tony," Ava had concluded in the letter. "And so does Mama."

He didn't like the sound of that. He didn't want his sister and mother growing attached to Rachel, even though he was growing attached to her, too. Mysteries and challenges intrigued him, he assured himself. That was her appeal. And the knowledge that he could help her professionally.

So, to keep the restlessness at bay, he'd been putting out feelers as well as calling in favors to see Rachel's design career properly launched. And he'd decided to bankroll some of her immediate expenses. Tonight, he was having dinner with Daphne Valero at one of his favorite restaurants in Rome. He'd had business dealings with Daphne in the past, as well as one very memorable personal interlude in Paris a few years earlier before she became the head of her family's perfume empire.

La Fleur Fragrances was based in her mother's native France, but also had offices in Rome, which was where her father had been born. The company was one of the Fortuna Publishing Group's most valued advertisers both in the United States and in editions of its magazines abroad. The company's signature scent, *Simply Timeless,* packaged as it was in a distinctive hourglass-shaped bottle, was carried in the most exclusive department stores and boutiques around the globe. Rachel would be targeting a similarly well-heeled clientele. To Tony's way of thinking, perfume and jewelry went hand in hand. Those who bought high-end fragrances also bought high-end jewelry.

Besides, Daphne adored jewelry, and as the heiress to a perfume empire, her likeness often wound up between the covers of magazines such as his, right along with the advertisements for La Fleur Fragrances. She wasn't only a businesswoman. She set trends. It would be a boon for Rachel if such an influential international fashion icon were to be seen and photographed wearing her designs.

"Tony!"

Daphne gave him an enthusiastic kiss on both cheeks when she arrived at the restaurant. He'd suggested meeting there, well aware of where the aperitif she had suggested in her invitation to cocktails at her apartment might lead.

"You look as lovely as ever," he said, pulling out a chair for her.

It was no empty compliment. Daphne was a beautiful woman, stylish and sleek, with a body whose curves could be every bit as dangerous as those of a racetrack. There was a time when he would have been eager to take those curves for a drive. But not this evening.

"I was happy to receive your message. It has been so long." Her voice grew huskier. "Much too long."

"Will you still be happy to see me if we discuss a bit of business?" he asked.

She left that open by replying, "It depends."

When the wine steward came by, he ordered a bottle of Piper Heidsieck.

"Are we celebrating?" Daphne asked.

He offered a careless shrug. "Do we need a reason to drink champagne?"

"None that I can think of." Her smile turned feline then. "Perhaps you are trying to ply me with alcohol so that you might take advantage of me later."

"I am too much of a gentleman for that."

"More's the pity."

They chatted a little bit about the changes his magazines—and the entire publishing world—were undergoing. Then he asked after her father, who had suffered a stroke the previous year. Tony waited until after their appetizer arrived to bring Rachel into their conversation.

"That is a lovely bracelet you are wearing."

"You like?" Daphne fussed with the clasp. "It belonged to my late grandmother."

"Some pieces are timeless. I know a designer whose jewelry would appeal to someone with your good taste."

"Is that so?" Daphne selected a piece of bruschetta. "Who?"

"She is largely unknown at this point."

"But you are hoping to change that," Daphne guessed.

"I am. She has designed several pieces for me in the past. I have always believed that her work deserved a larger forum, but at the time…" He shrugged. "She had other commitments."

"Is her work truly that good?"

"It is. I would not keep going back to her otherwise."

"Wouldn't you?"

Tony took a bite of his bruschetta in lieu of answering the question. After swallowing, he said, "Do you remember the necklace that Astrid was wearing at the after party in Milan last week?" He was betting Daphne did, since she'd stopped Astrid to admire it. At her nod, he said, "That was Rachel's."

Daphne puckered her lips. "I find myself a little jealous that we've never had a full-blown affair, Tony. I think I would have liked your parting gift."

He smiled. "So, you think she has talent, too."

"What I think is that it is a shame all I have to show from our one night together are some very erotic memories." She laughed, the same throaty sound he remembered from the evening in question. Then she grew serious. "It was a lovely piece. And cleverly designed with the way she set the aquamarine in fish-shaped prongs for Pisces."

"Yes. A bit of whimsy intended to pay homage to Astrid's interest in the zodiac."

"What exactly is it that you are you after, Tony?"

"Not much, really." He lifted his shoulders. "Someone who could help open doors for her. Rachel can do the rest."

Daphne pursed her lips. "And you think I can open those doors?"

"You are being modest. Beyond being a savvy businesswoman, you are very influential, Daphne. The kind of woman other women look to. You set the trends that the masses then follow."

"Is that the best you can do with your flattery?" But he could tell that, in addition to being flattered and amused, she was intrigued.

During the remainder of their meal, Tony laid out his idea for a publicity campaign that he believed would be mutually beneficial to Rachel and Daphne.

"One complements the other. Fine jewelry and a carefully crafted fragrance." He poured more champagne into her flute before lifting his own glass for what he hoped would be a pre-celebratory sip.

"And you are willing to give us discounted advertising space in *Moorings*," she said, referring to the Fortuna-owned magazine that appealed to the yachting set.

"I am. You have been a valued client."

Daphne's lips twitched, but then she asked, "Does she have a portfolio that I can see? As a savvy businesswoman, I cannot be expected to merely take your word."

"She is working on the portfolio now." If she wasn't, she would be as soon as Tony made a phone call. Daphne studied the bubbles in her flute. "I would like to meet her."

Much like the bubbles in the champagne, Tony felt excitement rise at her words. He told himself it was because his plan was coming together. His objective for the evening was met. That was the only reason he was feeling so elated.

"When?"

"I will be in New York for ten days starting next Wednesday. Can you arrange an introduction? Say on Friday evening?"

"Would Saturday be out of the question?"

Daphne pursed her lips again. "Because it is you asking, I will agree to Saturday."

"Grazie mille."

Dinner progressed, though it took longer to wind up than Tony expected. Of course, everything took longer in Italy. The country ran on its own time. Generally, that was how he liked it. He preferred to linger over each course and finish off the meal with espresso. Not this evening. This evening he was eager to call Rachel. Eager to give her the news. Eager simply to hear her voice.

That thought brought him up short.

As did Daphne's parting words an hour later as they stood outside the restaurant waiting for her limousine to arrive.

"I am curious to meet your little designer friend, Tony. Not only to see her work, but to see the woman who has you so eager to please her."

"That is not the way of things," he replied on a laugh.

"No?"

"No."

But Daphne looked as convinced as he felt.

FOR the past few weeks, Christmas sales had been keeping Rachel busy at the shop, as was overseeing the renovations upstairs. Construction work had slowed down considerably as the holidays approached. She tried not to worry about the delays, even when Will Daniels came down to her office the day before to report that a family emergency had prompted a city worker to reschedule the electrical inspection slated for the following Tuesday. Now, the inspection would have to be put off until after the first of the year. Until the work passed inspection, they could not begin to hang the drywall. So, one delay led to another.

It was probably just as well, she consoled herself.

Between her hours at the shop and working on jewelry sketches in the evening, she hadn't had time to meet with the kitchen designer to go over the final plans for cabinets. Nor had she picked out the light fixtures or moldings or... or...or. It seemed endless, especially since she'd revamped the blueprint once already to accommodate Tony's suggestion that she add in a space for her work.

She was lying in bed, wide-awake despite the fact that her alarm clock was not set to ring for another two hours, when the cell phone on the bedside table rang. Tony. She smiled.

"You're early," she teased upon answering.

"What do you mean, I am early?"

"Well, it's only ten after four here. You usually call between six-thirty and seven o'clock most mornings." She was out of the shower by then, dressed and downstairs having her morning coffee and a carton of yogurt. "I hate to break it to you, Tony, but you have become predictable."

She thought her use of the *p* word would have him sputtering in denial. His tone turned sinful instead. "I have caught you while you are still in bed, then. Describe for me what you are wearing. Do not skimp on the details."

Because her flesh began to prickle, she chided, "What if your mother was here?"

"If my mama was there, I would wonder what she is doing at my home this time of the morning and why she is in your bedroom." He chuckled. "So, what *are* you wearing?"

"Pajamas."

"I asked for details, *carina.* What do these pajamas look like? Are they made of silk? Are they edged in lace? How do they feel against your skin?"

"Like flannel," she replied drily. "Since that's what I'm

wearing. Red-and-green plaid with red satin piping on the cuffs and lapels. How's that for details?"

"Perhaps I will buy you some lingerie for Christmas. Something short and sheer."

She swallowed and did her best to ignore the pull low in her belly that his words inspired. "I don't think that would be a good idea."

"Why not? I could help you put it on. Then I could help you take it off."

"All kidding aside—"

"Who is kidding?"

She ignored him. "I probably should tell you that, as it is, Lucia is under the impression that something is, um, going on between the two of us."

He sighed heavily and his voice lost its flirtatious tone. "Is she still dropping by the house unannounced?"

"Unannounced? No," Rachel hedged.

"But she is stopping by."

"Now and then." In addition to the tiramisu recipe that his mother had penned longhand as Rachel sat in the Russos' dining room on Thanksgiving, Lucia had visited half a dozen times since their initial introduction. She called first, but she made it plain she was on her way and not seeking approval to come. She also had stopped by Expressive Gems the previous week. It was hard to be irritated when she'd left an hour later with several thousand dollars' worth of jewelry.

"I will speak to her," Tony was saying.

"That's not necessary." Rachel confided on a laugh, "She's teaching me how to cook, including all of your favorite dishes."

The revelation didn't garner the reaction she expected. Instead of laughing with her, Tony cursed. "I will speak to her," he said again.

"Really, Tony. I don't mind."

"But I do." His tone was resolute. Argument over, apparently, if indeed it could be considered an argument.

"Tony?"

He changed the subject. "How is the work progressing on your apartment?"

"It's hit a few snags," she admitted. She told him about the postponed electrical inspection. "The guys have been great, but Will warned me that since they have work to do at another site, it may be a little while before he can get his crew back to my place for the drywall."

"There is no rush, you know. I will not turn you out onto the streets if you still have need of my home when I return, *carina.*" The good humor was back in his tone.

Her gaze strayed to the pillow next to her in the bed. She could picture Tony there...smiling in that sinful way of his. Rachel threw off the covers and levered herself off the mattress, dropping the phone in her haste as she reached for the robe at the foot of the bed.

"Sorry. Are you still there?"

"I am here," Tony said. "But where are you?"

"Up." She tucked the cell phone between her ear and shoulder so she could belt the robe. "I'm heading downstairs."

"To the kitchen?"

"That will be the first stop. Once I set the coffee to brew, I think I'll go into the study. I like that room. It's cozy. I've been spending a lot of evenings in there working on my designs. I am feeling very creative lately," she confided.

"Good. Are you working on anything in particular?"

She reached the kitchen and flipped on the undercounter lighting, preferring its soft glow to the brighter overhead bulbs. "No, just something that I've been toying with ever since seeing a vase in a department store while doing some Christmas shopping."

"You found inspiration in a vase?"

She added water to the coffeemaker's reservoir and put ground coffee into a filter. "Not the vase itself, but the fluidity of the colors and the way they melded together."

"And you hope to replicate that how?" he asked.

She hit the on switch and leaned against the counter. "That's the question. I like the idea of different color gemstones dangling at different lengths from a choker, but…"

"That does not capture the sensuality you are after," he finished for her.

"Exactly."

Rachel couldn't recall ever having a conversation such as this with anyone. Certainly not with Mal. Nor with her mother or sister or even the women she employed at her shop. It wasn't only that she felt proprietary about her designs and unwilling to unveil them before they were fully conceived. She'd always considered the creative process a solitary venture, a maze to be maneuvered through on her own and at her own speed. But she appreciated Tony's input. Indeed, she was enjoying hearing his take. She told him so.

"Does this make me your muse?" he asked. She heard the smile in his voice, pictured that same smile denting his lean cheeks. It wasn't the smoldering bedroom variety. This smile was more intimate. She'd seen it a few times before he'd left the country. It had the same ruthless effect on her heart rate.

"I suppose in a way you are responsible for my most recent run of creativity, given the direction you are proposing to take my career."

"A perfect segue," he murmured. "Your career is why I am calling."

She tucked away the foolish pang of disappointment she felt that he wasn't calling merely to chat. Every call he'd made to her these last weeks ultimately had a purpose beyond the flirting with which it started out. Had a package arrived? Was the gate working properly? Had the company he'd hired been out to restring the outdoor Christmas lights that had blown loose during a storm? But, then, she was acting as his house-sitter. Tony may have made it plain that he wanted to sleep with her, but wanting to have sex wasn't the same as wanting a relationship. Besides, she wasn't in the market for one of those herself.

Business. She focused on that. "I'm all ears."

"I had dinner with a friend of mine who I believe might be able to help you."

As Tony went on about the particulars, Rachel felt her mouth drop open. His *friend* was Daphne Valero, the chic and lovely perfume heiress who had single-handedly helped the careers of a number of fashion designers simply by wearing their clothes. If Daphne was seen wearing it—shoes with a sequined vamp, an off-the-shoulder dress, a snakeskin clutch, a pair of owlish tortoise-shell sunglasses—they became the season's new must-haves.

"She has asked to meet you," Rachel heard him say over the buzzing in her head.

"She wants to meet me? What did you have to do to get her to say that?" She intended the question as a joke, but her imagination was busy filling in the blanks that, in truth, were none of her business to fill in.

Tony added fuel to the fire when he replied softly, "If you are truly curious, *carina,* I could arrange a demonstration for you."

"That won't be necessary." Even to her own ears, her tone sounded prim.

His answering laughter came as no surprise.

"So, when and where will this meeting take place?" she asked.

"If I said this weekend in New York, would that be a problem?"

"That's two days away."

"Have you other commitments?"

"The shop—"

"Jenny can handle it. She seems a competent enough young woman to me." Except when Tony was around, Rachel mused, at which point Jenny turned into an unproductive puddle of estrogen. "You have left her in charge before, no?"

"I have, but I already told her I would close on Saturday."

"No date this weekend, *carina?*"

Since he sounded so amused, she shot back with, "As a matter of fact, I do have plans."

Heidi was after her to have dinner with their father. On her own, Rachel had managed to dodge every invitation Griff extended. Heidi was harder to ignore and impossible to tell no, meaning Rachel had caved in. The only concession she'd managed to wring from her sister was that they meet for a late dinner at a popular restaurant rather than Heidi's apartment. Rachel wanted to keep the visit as brief as possible and that was more likely to occur at a busy eatery.

"With?" From Tony's smug tone it was clear that he didn't believe her.

"As it happens, a man." Which wasn't a lie. Her father might be a weasel, but he was a man.

"Ah. I did not realize." The words sounded curt.

Rachel couldn't quite put a finger on Tony's mood. Was he angry? Hurt? He had no reason to be. Just as she had no reason to wonder about what had occurred between him and Daphne Valero.

"That's because you didn't ask. You assumed." Feeling that she'd made her point, Rachel admitted, "The man in question is my father. Heidi wants the three of us to have dinner together, an early Christmas celebration."

"And you are okay with that?" he surprised her by asking.

"I'm doing it for Heidi."

"Take my advice, *carina,* and do it for yourself," was his sincere reply. "Bad blood between family, it is no good."

She cleared her throat, but before she could change the subject, he went on. "I had a disagreement with my father the day he died. He felt I was not applying myself to my studies. He reminded me that despite his wealth, I would have to make my own fortune one day if I wanted to continue to live the way I was."

So that was where Tony's drive came from. She doubted he was conscious of it.

He was saying, "Words were said that I could not take back later."

"Oh, Tony, you were only a boy."

"Yes, and I know he forgave me. But I would much rather have sought that forgiveness from him before he was gone."

"My father doesn't want my forgiveness."

"How can you be so sure? He has been around a lot lately. You have told me so yourself."

Could Tony be right? Years of hurt feelings made it hard to believe Griff had changed. She knew what was more likely: "He wants to assuage his conscience. That's not the same thing as seeking true forgiveness." She changed the subject. "Getting back to Daphne Valero, does the meeting have to be this weekend? I hate to sound ungrateful, but I need to budget for such an expense."

Rachel didn't have the money on hand to book a flight

to New York and stay in a hotel, especially on such short notice.

"Actually, it is next weekend. I was just curious what you were doing this weekend." He laughed softly. "As for budgeting, there is no need. In fact, I have already made all of the necessary arrangements."

In the next breath he was rattling off her flight itinerary. "A driver will be waiting for you at the airport to take you to your hotel. I will pick you up for cocktails at Delacorte's at six-thirty. Daphne will join us for dinner."

"You did all of this without consulting me?" She cleared her throat. Regardless of his motives, she needed to make something clear. "Listen, Tony, I truly appreciate everything you are doing on my behalf. You have been exceedingly generous and kind, but—"

"I should have included you in the decision-making process."

Rachel held her breath. She expected some argument. Tony was a man used to calling the shots and not having them questioned. So his ready agreement and quick apology came as a surprise.

"You are right. I am sorry. I should have asked before making the arrangements. You are not the sort of woman who likes being told what to do."

"I'm not. No." Tony had always made her aware of her femininity. Now, with that one statement, he had made her aware of her power. How interesting that it was not with pretty words and compliments that he managed to infiltrate her heart, but by expressing his understanding that she was his equal. "Thank you."

"In my excitement, I got ahead of myself."

"So, you're excited about this?"

"I am. Yes. It is a good opportunity for you. Will the following weekend work or shall I reschedule your flight?

I should mention that Daphne will only be in New York for a limited time. As will I. I am hoping to make the most of that time."

"What do you mean?"

"I know a buyer for an upscale department-store chain. In our last conversation I mentioned to her that I knew a fabulous up-and-coming jewelry designer who was looking to expand her clientele and was willing to let the chain's flagship New York store host her spring collection's debut."

Rachel's breath caught in her throat. What he described sounded like something straight out of her dreams. Unfortunately, reality intruded. "I don't have a spring collection."

"But you will," he replied confidently. "I'm going to arrange an introduction to her, as well. What do you think?"

"I think I need to sit down."

His laughter followed. "So, you will come?"

"How can I possibly say no?"

"And the arrangements that I have made, they are amenable to you, then? Flight times can be changed if need be."

Her heart warmed at his deferential tone. He wasn't merely humoring her. "They work. But, Tony, I will pay you back."

"I consider it an investment, but as you wish."

Her dreams were coming true and he was largely responsible for that—not only because of his connections and money, but because he believed in her. He made her believe in herself.

"Tony, I don't know what to say."

"Say that you have more than a couple of fabulous pieces on hand that you can show Daphne when you come."

Rachel laughed. "I do. Well, sort of. I'll have to ask to borrow them back from the people I've given them to as gifts over the years." That included her mother, sister and some of her friends.

Rachel pulled her feet out from beneath her on the couch. She felt the need to have them planted firmly on the floor while her imagination took flight.

She made a mental inventory, excitement building as she catalogued each ring, necklace, bracelet and set of earrings. Some of her early pieces were too amateurish to include, but there was enough there for an adequate representation of her ability, especially if she was able to finish the piece she was working on now.

"Are you still there?" An amused voice asked.

"Sorry. Just thinking."

"I have given you much to consider. Go back to bed."

"As if I could sleep now," she replied on a laugh.

Tony wasn't laughing, nor did she get the feeling he was talking about the upcoming meeting when he said, "I know what you mean."

CHAPTER NINE

RACHEL had much to do and little time in which to do it.
She resigned herself to the fact that the apartment renovations were behind schedule and would remain so until
after the holidays. For now, she had other matters to worry
about, and chief among them were the upcoming meet-
ings with Daphne and Shay Stevens, the Zindal's department-store buyer Tony had mentioned in his call. Rachel
would be having Sunday brunch with her before returning to Michigan.

In addition to borrowing the pieces she needed and
putting together a portfolio using the photographs she'd
taken over the years of the jewelry she'd designed, Rachel
decided a couple of new outfits were in order. Heidi came
shopping with her, which was both good and bad.

Good, because her sister was more likely to talk her into
something than out of it, and bad for that very same reason.

By the time Rachel left the collection of stores at
Somerset, she could barely fit all of her purchases in the
trunk of her car. She had more than a couple of outfits
and the accessories to go with them. She had lingerie.
She never should have allowed Heidi to draw her in to
Victoria's Secret.

"Black is sexy," Heidi remarked as she took a lace-
edged demicup bra from a rack.

"I don't think I'm Daphne Valero's type," Rachel had quipped. "Nor that of Shay Stevens."

"It goes to confidence."

"And that bra is going to make me feel confident?" She said it as a question and pretended to be doubtful, even though she knew the sexy scrap of support would indeed make her feel confident in ways unrelated to work.

She'd gone along, buying the bra's twin in white, and matching panties for both, because, well, it seemed like sacrilege to pair such nice bras with unbecoming cotton. As for the nightgown she purchased, she couldn't blame Heidi for talking her into that and her sister's wide, knowing smile said as much.

Rachel knew she still didn't look the part of an up-and-coming jewelry designer with her mousy, unstyled locks and ragged cuticles, so even though time was at a premium as the days ticked down to her trip, she fit in a visit to the salon to see both her stylist and the nail technician. Three hours later, she walked out the door of Tresses sporting streaky blond highlights and a stylish cut, not to mention a French manicure on both her fingernails and her toenails.

Several days later, wearing wide-legged gabardine trousers and a fitted white blouse, under which one of the new bras was making the most of her assets, she waited for Heidi to take her to the airport. The car that arrived at Tony's home, however, belonged to her father. She was tempted not to open the gate for him. She did, but she was waiting along with her luggage under the portico when his car reached the house.

"This is some place, kitten." Griff issued a low whistle as he glanced around.

"I'm house-sitting," came her clipped reply.

"So you said the other night at dinner. You didn't mention you were staying at a mansion. I was picturing a nice little bungalow like the kind your mom and I lived in when you were a kid."

Back before he broke up their family with his infidelity.

"What are you doing here, Dad?"

"Taking you to the airport. Heidi called in a panic. She couldn't make it. Something came up last minute and she asked me to pinch-hit for her." He offered his best salesman's smile. "I'm only too happy to help out my girls."

Except for when it wasn't convenient for him, Rachel thought. She didn't want Griff there. She was nervous enough already. She'd been looking forward to her sister's cheery chatter and unflagging support to send her on her way. She didn't want to spend the next forty minutes in a car with Griff, tiptoeing around the scores of landmines that dotted their personal histories.

Dinner the previous Saturday had been enough of a trial. Griff, of course, had insisted on paying for her meal even after she'd made it plain that she didn't want him to do so. She'd ordered chicken Florentine, since it was one of the most affordable items on the menu, and a glass of iced tea. Griff wasn't satisfied with that. Oh, no.

"We're celebrating, kitten."

He'd asked the waitress to bring lobster tails for all three of them and then ordered a bottle of Medallion Winery's award-winning chardonnay.

"I don't drink, Dad."

Heidi had even backed her up on that. "Yeah, Rach's face gets all red and blotchy whenever she does."

"A sip won't hurt. It's been so long since the three of us have sat down together for a meal."

When the wine came, he poured her a glass. It went untouched, as did her lobster tail. She'd left the restaurant irritated and, to her dismay, sad. Her father didn't know her at all. What's more, he didn't appear interested in the adult she'd become.

His insistence on calling her kitten was a prime example. She'd hated that nickname as a kid. At thirty-two, she absolutely loathed it. But he used it again now as he opened the tiny trunk of his sports coupe and lifted her bags into it.

"I like what you've done with your hair, kitten."

"I just had it trimmed. And highlighted," she mumbled.

"Well, you look pretty." He gave the ends an affectionate tug, making her feel twelve, except that when she was twelve her Dad hadn't been around.

"Thanks."

"Heidi tells me the guy who owns this grand home is interested in you."

"Tony is just a friend."

"Does he feel that way, too, that he is *just* a friend?" Griff's brows rose.

Rachel was unable to hold her father's gaze. Tony had made it plain that he wanted much more from her than mere friendship or a business relationship. Meanwhile, she hadn't made up her mind how far she intended to let anything personal between them go, the fact that she was wearing sexy, lace-trimmed undergarments aside. It was complicated, especially since he was helping her launch her design business on a much grander scale. He might claim one had nothing to do with the other, but having just gone through a divorce, she knew only too well that people sometimes made promises they did not keep. She hadn't confided her concerns in her sister. She certainly wasn't going to confide them in her here-today, gone-tomorrow father.

"Look, Dad, I appreciate your concern—"

"No, you don't," Griff interrupted. Despite his smile,

his expression was surprisingly sad. "You tolerate it, but you don't appreciate it. I'm worried about you, okay? Some guys, well, they expect to be repaid for their kindness, if you know what I mean."

Rachel didn't want to be touched by her father's concern. She didn't want her father's concern, period.

"I'm thirty-two years old, Dad. I think I can take care of myself." She slammed the trunk closed. The sound echoed across the frozen yard.

"You probably can. God knows, I wasn't around enough to look out for you when you were a teenager," he replied on a sigh as he shoved a hand back through his hair. When had it become so gray? He was saying, "Or when you got engaged to Mal."

"What's Mal got to do with anything?" she ground out.

"He wasn't good enough for you."

"You're right," she agreed with a quick dip of her chin. "Mal wasn't good enough for me. But how would you know, Dad? As you said, you weren't around."

Oh, the next time she saw Heidi, Rachel was going to kill her. *Something came up.* Right. What came up was her sister's meddling.

Griff surprised Rachel by saying, "Mal is the kind of man who insists on coloring inside the lines and expects others to do the same. That's the kind of man your mother needed. But not you." He reached out and chucked her under her chin. "You need someone who paints in big, bold strokes and isn't afraid to go off the paper every now and again—never mind about staying inside the damned lines."

She had to agree, but...

"Dad—"

Griff wasn't finished. "I've messed up a lot, and I've missed out on a lot as a result. I'm sorry for that."

"Dad, please." Rachel shook her head. She didn't

want to get into this now, even as Tony's words about her father's motives were ringing in her head. She didn't have the emotional fortitude or the time. "I need to get to the airport."

She walked around to the passenger side of the car and got in, hoping that would be the end of it. Griff, however, wasn't going to be put off. As soon as he was seated behind the leather-wrapped steering wheel, he said, "Heidi has always been the easier of the two of you to win over."

Buy off, he meant.

"That's because Heidi was a toddler when you walked out and she doesn't remember Mom crying all the time and making excuses for you when you failed to show up for holidays and birthdays and every school function."

Her sister had never had a father who could be counted on to show up. For a brief time, Rachel had.

Griff waited until they were out in traffic to say, "God, I really screwed up."

Let it go, let it go, she chanted silently. Instead, she hollered, "Yes, Dad. You did! You screwed up royally."

A muscle worked in his jaw. He didn't look angry. He looked frustrated and…old. Where had those deep grooves that bracketed his mouth come from?

"Do I get another chance, kitten?"

"Call me kitten again and no." She folded her arms over her chest and turned to stare out her window. Confused by her father's seeming sincerity and nervous about the upcoming trip, Rachel did her best to ignore Griff for the rest of the ride to Metro.

When they reached the airport half an hour later, Griff started to change lanes so he could pull into the short-term parking lot.

"There's no need for that, Dad. Just drop me at my airline's curbside luggage check-in. That way you won't have to pay for parking."

"I don't mind."

"Please. It will save time and money."

She thought the explanation would appeal to him. He was a man who had never cared to be short on either. But he seemed disappointed when he said, "All right."

He helped her with her luggage and, despite a security guard's reminder that he couldn't park the car there, Griff appeared to be in no hurry to leave her.

It was cold outside, and unlike her, he wasn't wearing gloves. He brought his hands to his mouth and blew on them. "Got everything?"

"Yes. Thanks for the ride." She started to turn, but he laid a hand on her arm.

"Have a safe trip, kit—Rachel." He caught himself with a sheepish smile. "Knock 'em dead with your designs."

It was impossible not to feel pleasure at his words. What child didn't want the approval of a parent, even one who had proved so unreliable? Her smile was genuine, if a little surprised, when she replied, "Thanks."

TONY waited amid a shuffling crowd of people eager to welcome guests or returning loved ones at LaGuardia. He nearly missed Rachel when she deplaned. At first, his gaze skipped right over the stylish young woman with the streaky blond hair. She was wearing a bright red belted tunic top over a pair of trousers, with a black trench coat slung over one arm and pulling a hard-sided wheeled carry-on case that was decorated in zebra stripes. When his gaze zipped back, Rachel's red-glossed lips were curved in a self-satisfied grin.

Her hair was down. It fell about her shoulders in careless waves that made his hands itch to touch it.

She looked lovely, chic. Her wide smile told him that she knew it. She'd never lacked for confidence when it came to her shop. This sort of confidence was different, rooted in her femininity. It looked incredibly sexy on her.

His heart did a quick *knock-knock* that he couldn't explain and hadn't experienced in ages, if ever. He started toward her through the crowd, impatient to reach her.

When he finally did, he said, "Welcome to New York."

"Tha—"

That was as far as he let her get before tugging her into his arms for a kiss, during which the hustle and hurry of the other travelers was forgotten. Tony couldn't get enough of her. She tasted as good as she looked and felt even better with that slim body pressed snug against his. A surprising amount of need welled up inside of him, surprising because not all of it was sexual. He drew away. Slowly. The busy terminal came back into focus. As did Rachel's expression. It held a mixture of surprise and desire with a little trepidation thrown in. He knew exactly how she felt.

"Wh-what was that for?" she asked softly.

I have missed you.

Madonna mio! He caught himself before he said the words.

"You are so beautiful," he replied instead, falling back on his usual flattery. "I could not help myself."

"I finally found time for a visit to my salon this week." She shrugged, but the smug smile was back in place.

"So I see. Very nice, *carina.* Very nice."

He took a step back and made a thorough study of her, starting with the blond highlights and ending at the pointy-toed high heels on her feet. She looked sophisticated, successful and every inch a woman thanks to the flattering fit of the clothes, which defined her tidy curves.

Because he was tempted to drag her back in for a second long kiss, Tony said, "I have a car waiting. Dinner is not until seven, so I thought, since the restaurant is not far from my apartment, we could stop there and use the time to go over your designs before then. How does that sound?"

"Fine." But she hesitated. "Where will I be staying, Tony? You never said."

"You are welcome to stay with me. I have a big bed." The flush in her cheeks could be taken a couple of ways. He went with the one most flattering to his ego. Smiling, he added, "Or, if you do not trust yourself, you could stay in my guest room."

"Tony—"

"I am teasing, *carina*." Though he hadn't been. Not completely. Part of him had been hoping, he realized. "I have made reservations for you at a hotel not far from Times Square."

She moistened the lips he wanted to kiss again. "Would you mind taking me there now? I'd like to check in and get settled."

"As you wish."

Forty-five minutes later, Tony's driver stopped the Mercedes sedan at the guest entrance to the Cavanaugh Arms. One of the hotel's bellmen hurried out with a brass trolley to help with Rachel's bags, but there was no need. She packed light enough for the two of them to handle everything. In addition to the smart little carry-on, she had only a garment bag.

Rachel would be staying the weekend, but many of the women Tony knew would have packed double, even triple what she had for an overnight stay. He said as much as they stood in one of the hotel's glass elevators, streaking toward the thirty-ninth floor.

"Actually, I brought four changes of clothes in addition to what I have on right now."

"I like this outfit. The tunic in particular. The color is very becoming on you. Is it new?"

She nodded. "In addition to having my hair done, I found time for a shopping trip. Heidi came with me. My sister is a bad influence. On top of clothing suitable for business, she talked me into... Well, a lot of other stuff." Rachel turned away, pretending to be absorbed in the stunning view of the atrium, but not before he saw her blush again.

What exactly had her sister talked Rachel into buying? Given her rosy cheeks, Tony decided it had to be something he would enjoy seeing firsthand.

EVEN before they entered her hotel room, Rachel knew she'd made a mistake. She should have agreed to go to Tony's apartment. While that hadn't seemed a wise choice at the time, at least there they wouldn't have been confronted by the specter of a king-size bed the moment they walked through the door.

He took her coat, shed his own.

As he hung them in the closet, she walked to the wall of windows and parted the blinds. Far down below, the spectacle that was Times Square pulsed with people and action. She was eager to see it that evening, all lit up, with its huge billboards hawking everything from diet cola to luxury cars and golf clubs.

"This is a nice room, very spacious," she added, even though at the moment it felt as if the walls were closing in on them.

"It has a very nice bed, too," Tony remarked.

She turned to find him sitting on the dove-gray satin

duvet, his grin every bit as sexy as the underwear she was trying to forget she had on beneath her clothes.

"So, do you want to see my designs?" She reached for her oversize purse. Most of the borrowed jewelry was inside it. She was wearing the rest: a ring, necklace and earrings. She hadn't wanted to take the chance of losing any of it.

His mouth curved into a smile that was the perfect complement to his bedroom surroundings. "Will you show me your etchings, too? That is the cliché, no?"

She laughed because that was what he expected. Then she cleared her throat. "I think we need to get something out of the way."

"I was thinking that very thing." Again the smile appeared, but then he sobered and stood. "You are going to tell me that ours is a business arrangement only. For now."

The two words he added at the end didn't sound as ominous as they did exciting.

"Yes." She sucked in a breath before tacking them on to her response. "For now."

"I could change your mind."

"I know you could," she admitted.

Indeed, it wouldn't take much effort on his part. She was alone with him in a sumptuous hotel room, far from home and her normal routine. She was wearing new clothes, standing just beyond the precipice of that new chapter Heidi had assured her she would write. After that toe-curling kiss at the airport, Rachel found it was ever so tempting to give in to the attraction that had only grown stronger these past several weeks. Without realizing it, she took a step toward Tony.

"That is not what I want." His voice was oddly strained. The words smacked her in the face like ice water.

"You've decided you don't want me?"

He swore. First in English and then in Italian. At least she assumed the second word was an oath from the way he spat it out.

"I want you. Never doubt that. But I do not want you to have regrets after we make love. No recriminations."

Nor would he want any strings, which, given where she was in her life, should have sounded ideal. Her rebound man. Her reentry point into the world of dating. But was that all he would be? Was she capable of drawing a line and standing firm once she reached it? She knew Tony was.

"I think I should go before we both have regrets." He took his overcoat from the closet. The clang of hangers punctuated his brisk movements.

"Tony, I apologize for the mixed signals I've been sending. I—"

"No apology is necessary. It is all right, *carina*." But his smile failed to reach his eyes. "I will send a driver for you later. We can meet at the restaurant an hour ahead of Daphne's arrival and go over your designs then."

Before she had a chance to say anything else, he was gone.

Outside the hotel, Tony sucked in the crisp air before dismissing his driver. It was a long walk to his apartment, but he needed the exercise. He started up Broadway, his stride long, his steps quick. Even though he knew exactly where he was going, he'd never felt more lost. Why was he pursuing Rachel this way? What was it about the woman that made him so desperate to possess her? He pondered both questions all the way home, but was still seeking answers when he arrived.

Before leaving for Delacorte's, Rachel freshened her makeup and fussed with her hair, putting it up only to take it back down. Nerves fluttered in her belly every time she thought of the evening to come, and not only because she would see Tony again. She was dining with Daphne Valero, one of the most influential women in the fashion world.

It was hard not to feel like Cinderella, especially when Rachel stepped into her new dress. Afterward, as she examined herself in the hotel's full-length mirror, she was glad she had caved in to Heidi's nagging and bought some outrageously priced red heels. They were better than a pair of glass slippers any day, even if they felt about as comfortable at the moment. It had been a while since Rachel had worn anything other than practical flats and kitten heels.

As for the dress, it was a basic black sheath with three-quarter-length sleeves. She'd gone for simplicity on purpose. The dress was the perfect backdrop for the necklace she'd chosen. It was her design, of course, and one of her favorite pieces. She'd created the star-shaped blue moonstone pendant that hung from a box-link gold chain for Heidi for her college graduation. The gems weren't the best quality and the gold was fourteen carat rather than the eighteen that most of her paying clients requested. Rachel hadn't been able to afford either. Still, she felt that the overall representation of her work was spot-on. The piece managed to be sophisticated and whimsical at the same time thanks to the setting. Besides, Heidi claimed it was good luck.

With that in mind, Rachel hurried downstairs to meet Tony's driver. She had a date with destiny, as the saying went. She tried not to think about how Tony figured into it.

Tony couldn't have been more proud of Rachel when he watched her walk into the lounge at Delacorte's. It wasn't only her stylish clothes or the flattering hairstyle. It was the way she held herself, the confidence in her stride. Her very presence was that of a woman who knew she was going places. If she was nervous, she was hiding it well. He was on his feet and crossing to meet her even before the hostess pointed him out. Unlike at the airport, this time he contented himself with a peck on her cheek. After their conversation in her hotel room, he knew better than to press his control.

"You take my breath away, *carina*." He meant it.

"Thank you."

They took their seats. A server came by to refill Tony's coffee. Rachel ordered a cup of hot tea.

"About what happened at the hotel earlier," she began once they were alone again.

He shook his head before she could finish and laid a hand overtop of hers on the table. "Let's put that behind us."

"Can we do that?" She looked doubtful and as confused as he felt.

For her sake even more so than his own, Tony nodded. "It is all a matter of timing. I was wrong to try to rush things. When you are ready, you will let me know. Until then, I can be patient."

The words cost him. Part of him wanted Rachel out of his system. Surely, a sexual affair would accomplish that much. And if it didn't? He ignored the question and worked up a reassuring smile.

Tapping her portfolio, he said, "Now let me see what you have been up to these past weeks, *carina*."

Two weeks later, even with a symphony of hammering going on overhead, Rachel's spirits remained high. Her trip to New York had proved an unqualified success. Daphne Valero had not only been enthusiastic about what she saw in Rachel's portfolio, she'd placed an order for a necklace on the spot.

Asked what she wanted, the perfume heiress had waved one jewel-bedecked hand and announced in a thickly accented voice, "You are the designer. Surprise me."

Usually that kind of latitude would have pleased Rachel. Given all that was at stake, however, it had left her terrified. But only for about a week. Then late one night as freezing snow tapped at the windowpane keeping her awake, inspiration struck. She'd pulled back the covers and reached for her sketchbook. When Rachel had returned to bed just before dawn, she knew she'd nailed it. The two-inch amulet was shaped like an hourglass, representing La Fleur Fragrances' signature scent. The amulet opened and would hold a few drops of the perfume when all was said and done.

Despite the noise coming from upstairs, Rachel eagerly got to work now insetting tiny stones on the hourglass's top and base. She'd gone with rose-cut mixed sapphires. Tony agreed with her that they played into the romance of the piece. She'd spoken to him about her sketch not long after finishing it, even going so far as to email him a scanned copy. She still found it a little perplexing how much she shared with him when it came to her work. Not to mention how much she shared with him about things that had nothing to do with jewelry designing at all.

They spoke every day. Sometimes twice a day, despite the time difference. And there were emails. Since New York, he'd taken to signing them, "Yours patiently, Tony." The first time, he'd added a winking smiley-face icon. She had appreciated his attempt at levity, but they both knew what he was waiting patiently for. As the days passed, he wasn't the only one living in a state of anticipation. It was a wonder she got any work done.

As it was now, Rachel nearly dropped one of the sapphires before she could add it to the setting. Eventually, when she had the resources, she would have other people to help see her designs through from the sketching phase to finished product. For now, she was content to do it herself.

That included the pieces Shay Stevens had commissioned at their meeting the day after Rachel's dinner with Daphne. Shay, too, had raved about Rachel's work. Both women's reviews had further bolstered her confidence.

"You are going places," Tony had said smugly as they left the restaurant for the airport that brisk Sunday in December.

"Only because you are taking me." She'd sent him a grateful smile that had him shaking his head.

"No, *carina*. This is all you."

And Rachel still had to prove herself. She'd won over Shay and Daphne—no small feat in either case. But to truly be a success, her designs had to sell to a broader, albeit exclusive, consumer base, one with discriminating tastes and a tighter rein on their wallets these days.

Tony's idea for launching a spring collection, even for the following year, had proved too ambitious. Rachel did not want to rush the production of her debut line of fine jewelry, even though Shay had been specific about which pieces from Rachel's portfolio and sketchbook she felt would go over well with Zindal's deep-pocketed clientele.

Besides, a large-scale publicity campaign needed to be crafted with glossy, full-color ads in all of the hottest women's magazines. That took time to create and implement. The goal was to ensure that every fashionista and fashionista-wannabe on both sides of the Atlantic had heard of Rachel before anything actually went on sale in a single Zindal's store.

Some people, such as Daphne and a small circle of her

high-end friends, weren't willing to wait until then, of course. Daphne had made it clear she wanted Rachel to deliver her commissioned jewelry in person to her home in Rome, at which time Rachel would also have her first, if unofficial, "trunk show."

Usually, trunk shows were held at major retailers, such as Zindal's. That chain would be hosting the first wave of her shows in the United States at its stores nationwide once the collection went public. Trunk shows also were scheduled for a handful of select boutiques, including La Fleur Fragrances' Beverly Hills store on Rodeo Drive.

Rachel would be making personal appearances along with her jewelry. Models in her employ would be on hand as well, wearing her pieces and answering questions. Models! Wearing her work! Rachel's only stipulation to Tony was that Astrid not be among them.

Rachel didn't want to know what the budget for everything, including an international advertising blitz, was going to be in the end. Tony was taking care of everything from fronting the bill to overseeing the campaign created by the agency he had hired on her behalf. Rachel would have the final say, but for now she was happy to leave the details to him.

At her insistence, however, he had agreed to have a lawyer draw up an official contract outlining their partnership and the percentage of profits to which he was entitled until such time as Rachel was able to buy out his initial investment. She felt better knowing that everything was spelled out in black and white and had now been signed, witnessed and dated.

Of course, their relationship routinely lapped over the bounds set out by that contract. She didn't mind. Not in the least. All in all, Rachel decided, it boggled the mind how quickly her life was changing.

At her feet, a fluffy ball of gray and white fur meowed and rubbed insistently against her ankle.

"In a minute," she said with a laugh. "You are way too impatient."

The cat was a gift from Tony. On Christmas Day, while she had been at her mother's with Heidi having dinner, he'd popped in at his house and left the cat in a bow-wrapped animal carrier in her bedroom. He'd stopped in earlier, too, on his way to his mother's from the airport. He'd looked tired, but no less handsome. She'd given him his gift then, a pair of sand-dollar-shaped cufflinks, her design of course, that served as a thank-you as well as a Christmas present.

"They are wonderful." He'd immediately swapped out the pair on his French cuffs. "What do you think?"

"You will be the envy of all your friends," she'd teased.

"You say that in jest, but I believe it to be true."

He'd left then, telling Rachel that her gift would be delivered later. And it had been.

The card accompanying the cat read, "I saw him on an internet site for abandoned pets and could not resist. He needs a good home. You need companionship and a muse in my absence. I thought you could name him Fido, since you really should have a dog. In the meantime, he can keep you company during those long days at the shop."

It had been mutual love at first site. She hadn't taken Tony's suggestion for a name. Instead of Fido, she'd gone with Francis, after the patron saint of animals, since this one had been rescued, and from the looks of him not a moment too soon.

The cat had nicks on the points of both ears and a bald patch that had yet to fill in on his tail, suggesting he'd spent some time fighting in alleys before winding up at a shelter. The first time she'd petted him, she'd been able to feel every ridge in his spine as she'd run her hand over his back. He'd been that emaciated. He'd put on half a dozen pounds since then, and even though she hadn't planned to bring him to the shop until she could move in to the overhead apartment, she hadn't been able to bear leaving him alone all day in Tony's big house. Francis had become a fixture at the shop and a hit with the customers. He'd also inspired a couple of whimsical designs—a smooth, gold pendant of a cat licking its paw and a ring in which an eighteen-carat-gold cat stretched around the finger.

The fact that Tony had gone to the online rescue site rather than purchasing a fancy, flat-faced purebred that could double as a show animal came as somewhat of a surprise. But perhaps it shouldn't have. More and more, Rachel was realizing what a good heart Tony had. A soft one. Packaged in a body that could tempt a saint to sin.

Rachel was no saint.

She reached down to scoop up Francis. Once in her arms, the cat started to purr and began kneading her breast with his front paws before settling in.

"Did Tony teach you that?" she asked on a laugh.

Francis gazed up at her with eyes that were nearly the same rich hazel color as his benefactor's. She swore the cat winked.

▲ **The Reader Service—Here's how it works:** Accepting your 2 free books and 2 free gifts (gifts valued at approximately $10.00) places you under no obligation to buy anything. You may keep the books and gifts and return the shipping statement marked "cancel". If you do not cancel, about a month later we'll send you 6 additional books and bill you just $4.09 each for the regular-print edition or $4.59 each for the larger-print edition in the U.S. or $4.49 each for the regular-print edition or $5.24 each for the larger-print edition in Canada. That is a savings of at least 14% off the cover price. It's quite a bargain! Shipping and handling is just 50¢ per book in the U.S. and 75¢ per book in Canada.* You may cancel at any time, but if you choose to continue, every month we'll send you 6 more books, which you may either purchase at the discount price or return to us and cancel your subscription.

*Terms and prices subject to change without notice. Prices do not include applicable taxes. Sales tax applicable in N.Y. Canadian residents will be charged applicable taxes. Offer not valid in Quebec. Credit or debit balances in a customer's account(s) may be offset by any other outstanding balance owed by or to the customer. Please allow 4 to 6 weeks for delivery. Offer available while quantities last. All orders subject to credit approval. Books received may not be as shown.

▲ **If offer card is missing write to: The Reader Service, P.O. Box 1867, Buffalo, NY 14240-1867 or visit www.ReaderService.com**

CHAPTER TEN

ONE week together under the same roof. That was all it was, Tony reminded himself, as the hired limousine sped away from Detroit Metro. Surely, he could handle that.

Besides, it was his fault more so than the contractor's that Rachel's move to the apartment was delayed. Back in February, Tony had called Will from Rome and changed the order for the bathroom floor and shower stall, substituting the more economical porcelain tiles she'd selected for Carrara marble similar to what was found in his master bathroom. Now it was late March and his "housewarming gift" remained on backorder.

Rachel wasn't happy. He suspected it wasn't his high-handedness that ruffled her feathers, but the fact that after months of talking on the telephone, they would now be doing so face-to-face. In the morning and at night. For a solid week.

Santo cielo! What had he gotten himself into?

"Can you turn down the heat, *per favore?*" he asked the driver.

Tony was roasting, and he knew that only part of his elevated temperature could be blamed on the change in climate. Rome's weather was milder year round than Michigan's, but winter in both places had turned into spring. The romantic in Tony loved the season for what it represented. Leaves were budding, flowers were starting to bloom, and the male and female of various species were pairing off.

Meanwhile, he hadn't paired off with anyone in months. The only woman he was interested in bedding, or being with in any capacity for that matter, was Rachel. He'd turned down some very obvious overtures from some very beautiful women since the previous fall—women who would require no wooing beforehand and seek no strings after a physical affair. To their dismay and his increasing sexual frustration, he'd declined each and every one. He wasn't interested in what they had to offer. Rachel was on his mind twenty-four hours a day, seven days a week.

In addition to their professional association and growing attraction, which he knew to be mutual, they were moving in to virgin territory, at least for him. They shared a brand of intimacy Tony had never allowed himself to experience with a woman. For that matter, he hadn't known it existed. Even with his fiancée, Kendra, all those years ago, he hadn't been this emotionally open or felt this exposed. It was terrifying at times, but addictive. He kept wanting more, craving it as much as he needed it.

Meanwhile, his self-imposed celibacy was killing him. Would it end soon? He hoped so, but he couldn't be sure, even if some of their phone conversations became downright erotic at times. Still, he'd promised to leave the decision to Rachel. He'd also promised to be patient. The virtue was in short supply. His gaze skimmed over the passing landscape. He could only hope that if Rachel was not ready, he would have enough patience to see him through not only the week they would be under one roof, but the full month he would be in Michigan. After that, he would be back in New York for a couple weeks before heading to Rome, and then distance would suffice. Distance and more phone conversations, even the tamest of which had the ability to twist him into knots.

Tony unbuckled his seat belt long enough to shuck off his overcoat. Then he loosened the half-Windsor knot of his tie. To the driver he said, "Maybe you could switch on the air conditioning for a few minutes."

During the past several months, as he'd traveled around Europe and jetted between New York and Rome, he'd continued to call Rachel at the shop most days. He knew the status of her design work. That was business and she was a stickler for keeping him apprised of the details. She sent him regular updates via email, as well, attaching scanned images of her sketches. She was still doing them freehand even though he'd bought her some software that he'd thought she might find helpful. She claimed it hindered her creative process.

He sent her emails, as well. Some business-related, some not. All signed *Yours Patiently,* which had started out as a poor attempt at humor. Long ago, he'd realized the joke was on him.

As for the phone calls when he caught her at his home in the mornings, those centered on more personal matters. He found it surprisingly easy to tell her things, from the silly and mundane—he'd spilled espresso down the front of his shirt during a meeting—to more weighty matters—*Moorings* magazine's subscriptions were down along with advertising revenue and he was worried the changeover to internet content wasn't catching on fast enough to suit readers.

In return, he enjoyed listening to her days' happenings, and the latest installment of what was going on in regard to her relationship with her father. Much to her surprise, Griff was still in town and still coming around.

"Could it be he's really changed?" Tony had asked during one recent conversation.

She'd scoffed at that notion, though her denial had seemed more automatic than certain. "Leopards don't change their spots, Tony."

"Everyone changes." It had been suddenly important that she understood that.

When she'd said nothing, Tony had added, "Give your father the benefit of the doubt, *carina*. That is what I did with Paolo when he married my mother. He was a common laborer, not that there is anything wrong with that. But my father, he left our family well off thanks to his hard work and investments. I wondered if maybe Paolo was more serious about my mother's bank account than her."

"Oh, Tony. When I met Paolo at Thanksgiving it was so obvious that even now he is head over heels for Lucia."

"Obvious to you, yes. But to a young boy who was still grieving for his father…" He'd left it at that. "My point, Rachel, is that sometimes you have to move forward on faith."

Griff might not have changed completely, but Tony was willing to bet that with age he'd learned a few important lessons. The primary one being that his two daughters were adults now. They were no longer waiting eagerly for him to show up and grace them with his presence. They didn't need him. Griff had missed out on their childhoods. If he was to be part of their life at all, he was going to have to prove himself worthy. That meant coming around, even when his children weren't happy to see him. With Rachel especially, he would never be able to buy her affection.

Tony had enjoyed all of their phone calls over the past several months, but they were no substitute for seeing her in person. In the call he'd placed upon arriving in Detroit, she'd sounded eager to see him. He felt the same.

"Can you go any faster?" he asked the driver now.

It was just his luck that as soon as he said it, the traffic on I-75 began to back up.

The house was quiet when he finally arrived an hour later than he had planned. The mingling scents of oregano, garlic and simmering tomatoes greeted him as soon as he came through the door. It smelled like his mother's cooking. Was Lucia there, or had Rachel decided to show him how well she'd been paying attention to his mother's culinary lessons? He was hoping for the latter.

The cat appeared as Tony set down his suitcase and overcoat. The animal eyed him warily before making a pass around his legs. The contact was minimal but still left a trail of silvery-gray hairs on the charcoal gabardine.

"Hello, Fido. Are you the only one here to welcome me home?" He reached down to stroke the cat's back. The animal had put on weight since Christmas. Rachel's doing. When he straightened, she was there.

"Hi, Tony."

She smiled at him from half a dozen feet away. Her hands were clasped behind her back. She was the picture of restraint. Meanwhile, he ached to hold her. He chided himself for the foolish fantasy he'd entertained on the long plane ride home that she would rush into his arms the instant he walked through the door.

"I see you've become reacquainted with Francis," she said.

"He will always be Fido to me."

He removed his suit coat. It joined his trench on the rail of the curved banister. He shed his tie completely and flicked open the next two buttons on his shirt. All the while, Rachel's gaze followed his progress.

"I had hoped you would volunteer to do this for me," he said quietly.

"I know. I'd planned to."

She moistened her lips. He stifled a groan. "Then what are you doing way over there, *carina?*"

"Playing it safe," she admitted with a rueful shake of her head.

"I remember a woman telling me she had decided she was not going to do that any longer."

"Yes, well that was an easy decision to make at the time."

"But not now? Is that what you mean to tell me?" He smiled and knew a moment of triumph when she took a couple of steps in his direction.

"As if your oversized ego needs any further stroking."

"Perhaps not, but I have other parts, equally oversized, that could use a little attention."

He expected Rachel at least to smile. Instead, she sucked a deep breath through her teeth before nibbling on her plump bottom lip. If she wasn't as turned on as he was, she was doing an Academy Award–worthy imitation.

"I've missed you." Her voice shook.

"Then come here, *carina*," he all but begged. "Show me how much, and then I will return the favor."

She took one halting step forward. That was enough for Tony. He closed the distance between them in an instant, propelled by need as much as by impatience. After the first deep kiss, he rested his forehead against hers and fought to steady his breathing.

"It feels so good to hold you. All of those phone conversations, they were not enough. Never enough," he repeated in a whisper before kissing her again.

"Tony, about dinner—"

"It can wait. I have another appetite I am eager to satisfy at the moment. Tell me you feel the same way."

"I do, yes, but—"

"*Basta*. Enough. No more words." He'd had to content himself with those for months. Right now, he wanted to make love. His hands curved over Rachel's firm bottom. On a groan, he pulled her body flush against his, torturing himself as he imagined what it would feel like to be inside her. The soft moan that slipped from her lips was nearly his undoing. His bed was too far away. He started in the direction of the couch, his mouth still on hers.

"Let the poor girl come up for air, Antonio!"

His mother's voice had him jumping back. He glanced over to find Lucia and the rest of the family standing in the living room. Paolo, Bill and Ava were grinning. His mother, meanwhile, was trying to appear stern and offended. At ages two and four, his nieces weren't sure what to make of the fuss.

"Surprise," Rachel mumbled. Her face was as red as his mother's famed marinara.

He recovered quickly, some parts of him faster than others. "Look at this. My entire family. Here. Right now."

"You don't need to pretend to be happy to see us," Bill said, stepping forward to shake Tony's hand. "Rachel wasn't either when we descended on her like a pack of wolves less than an hour ago."

That earned Bill a poke in the ribs from Ava, who handed two-year-old Teresa to him so she could wrap Tony in a hug. "Mama thought it would be nice to surprise you with a home-cooked meal. I brought the bread and salad. She's responsible for the pasta and dessert." Her voice lowered. "Although I think Rachel might have that covered, too."

"So funny."

His sister laughed. "It is so good to see you."

"The same."

Just not right now. Still, Tony managed to shift gears.

The other, it could wait. His family would not stay long. He hoped. The look on Rachel's face told him she was hoping the same thing. He kissed the girls and greeted Paolo, saving his mother for last.

"Hello, Mama."

Her hug was fierce. Her words for his ears only, "I think you are more than business partners and I am not going to believe this *friends* nonsense."

She stepped back and clapped her hands together. "Come on, everyone. Into the dining room. Dinner is ready."

To Tony, Lucia said, "You go wash up." Clearing her throat, she added meaningfully, "And make yourself presentable."

Tony couldn't remember the last time he'd hosted a gathering of family around his dinner table. Despite his earlier pique over the interruption, he was happy to see everyone there.

"This marinara is part of a batch Rachel and I made last week. It is good, no?" Lucia said.

"Excellent," Paolo agreed.

Bill and Ava added their approval.

"What's marinara?" Maria wanted to know. Meanwhile, her little sister, Teresa, was finger painting with the sauce on her plate.

The adults all laughed, especially when Lucia gasped in mock dismay and said, "How can your daughter not know, Ava? By this age, she should be able to make it, too."

"Both girls will learn eventually. As will their little brother or sister." The dining room erupted in excitement almost before the words were out of Ava's mouth.

Tony glanced around. All of the women's eyes were moist, including Rachel's. For the next couple of minutes, happy tears were shed and hugs and backslaps were exchanged all around.

"Another grandchild." Lucia had dabbed her eyes with

her napkin as she settled back into her seat. "If your Papa were still alive, he would be so happy."

Paolo, who was seated next to Lucia, gave her arm an affectionate pat. "Yes, he would be. As am I."

It struck Tony anew what a good man his stepfather was. Paolo had been content to raise another man's children, loving and guiding them without ever trying to take their late father's place. What a gift it was that Lucia had been loved so deeply not once, but twice.

He glanced at his sister, intercepting the intimate smile she was sending to her husband of nearly a decade. Marriage, motherhood—both looked good on her. He credited Bill for that. He and Ava approached childrearing and all other facets of their life together as a team. They laughed a lot. No doubt they also fought. Ava was a Salerno, after all, as quick to argue as she was to forgive. Above all else, they loved one another—deeply, unabashedly and unconditionally.

It came as a bit of a shock to realize that he wanted exactly what Ava had. Every bit of it. The laughter and drama, the arguments and quiet mornings sharing coffee. The love-making that fulfilled more than physical needs. The security, the continuity, children to guide and raise, a family of his own.

Next to him, Rachel was asking Ava if they knew the baby's sex yet. As he listened to their very ordinary conversation, he knew he had to be sure. Rachel wasn't like Astrid and the long line of lovers who had shared his bed over the years. She was special, fragile in a way. Her marriage had ended in disaster less than a year ago. She was attracted to him, yes. And he wanted her as he had wanted no other woman. But what if he changed his mind? What if he made a commitment he could not keep? He refused to allow in the niggling worry that it might not be *his* mind he was concerned would change.

"I was beginning to think I would have to content myself with just two grandbabies to spoil." Across from him at the dinner table, Lucia cast a meaningful glance in Tony's direction.

To the surprise of all present, he replied, "Who knows what the future holds, Mama?"

Who indeed? A year ago, he had not seen himself going into business with Rachel, much less pursuing her romantically. He certainly hadn't imagined that she—or any other woman, for that matter—would be seated at his table, enjoying dinner with his family and looking as if she belonged there.

He remained uneasy about the bond forming between his mother and sister and Rachel. He couldn't bear to see them hurt if things didn't work out.

If. He mused over the word. For the longest time, it had been *when.* How right Tony was when he'd told Rachel that people could change.

The dishes were cleared from the table in preparation for dessert. His mother fussed over him and had Rachel fussing over him, as well.

"More tiramisu, Tony?" At his nod, Lucia told Rachel, who had already offered to go get the coffee, "Bring him a big piece."

He sent her a wink, but it turned out the joke was on him. An hour later, when his family was preparing to leave, Lucia said, "Tony, you will come with us."

"Come with you where?"

"Home." Lucia pointed to Rachel. "You cannot both stay here."

"Mama, I'm thirty-eight years—"

"I donna care how old you are. I donna care what you

have or have not done when I am not around. Until Rachel is in her apartment or there is a wedding band on her finger, you should not stay here. It is not proper."

"I can stay at my mom's," Rachel offered in a strangled voice. Her face was aflame.

Behind her, Ava and Bill were doing a poor job of trying to tuck away their smiles, but his sister did come to his defense.

"Mama, be reasonable. Tony has been on planes and in cars for the better part of the day. He's got to be exhausted."

He nodded his thanks.

Bill was less helpful. "I'm sure all Tony wants to do right now is climb in bed."

"His bed," Rachel inserted. "Alone." Her face was literally glowing by the time she finished.

"Rachel is right, Mama. I am too tired to seduce her." *Tonight,* he added silently, as exhaustion began to catch up with him. And even that might be negotiable once they were alone.

Begrudgingly, Lucia relented. "But no hanky-panky," she warned, shaking a finger in his face.

As his guests shuffled out the door a moment later, he heard Maria ask Ava, "What's hanky-panky?"

Tony closed the door and leaned against it. Rachel crossed her arms. "Too tired to *seduce* me? As if I would have no say in the matter."

"You are right." He held out his hand to her. Then, in the most arrogant tone he could muster, he added with a wink, "Come upstairs, *carina.* I will let you seduce me."

Tony woke the next morning confused. He was in his bed, but he was alone. A glance under the covers confirmed he was still wearing the same clothes he'd had on the day before, although his belt was gone and his shirt untucked. When he heard the light tap at the door, he shifted to a sitting position and called, "Come in."

Rachel opened the door and stepped inside. She was already dressed, outfitted for the shop.

"Sleep well?" she inquired.

He smiled sheepishly. "I did, but I have a feeling I drifted off at a most inopportune time."

"Oh, you drifted off even before then." But she chuckled after saying so.

This should be awkward, a blow to his masculinity even, Tony thought. But he fell back on his pillow and laughed instead. She came in to sit on the edge of the bed and joined him.

He reached for her right hand and fussed with the small peridot stone on a ring he'd never seen her wear before. Part of her growing collection, no doubt.

"Do I get a second chance?" He kissed the back of her hand. "Or have you come to your senses and decided not to sleep with me after all."

"No. I've made up my mind and it hasn't changed. I want you, Tony."

That statement didn't come as a surprise as much as a relief. But her next words caused him to suck in a breath.

"I believe you said last night that I could seduce you."

"I did."

"You also promised, back in December, to be patient."

He nodded. "And I have been. At great cost to my sanity, I might add."

She offered a smile he'd never seen before. It set his blood to boiling.

"Then you deserve a reward."

Rachel stood and, with hands trembling as much from anticipation as nerves, reached for the hem of her sweater.

She pulled it up slowly, stopping just for a moment when she reached the lacy bottom edge of her bra. She'd never seduced a man before, but the sound of Tony's ragged breathing told her she was doing a credible job of it. She pulled off the sweater in a flourish.

"Like what you see?" she asked. Was that husky voice really hers? When he started to reach for her, Rachel shook her head. "Remember, I'm doing the seducing."

She unzipped her skirt and shimmied out of it, leaving it in a puddle on the floor. Even as need clawed at her, she took her time. She wanted Tony every bit as desperately as he wanted her, but she also wanted this first encounter to be memorable. For both of them.

"I am eager to find out what piece of clothing you will remove now."

Only two were left and both covered very little. But the one she chose was his shirt. Knees on the bed, she straddled him. The night before she'd gotten through four buttons before his eyes had drifted closed. She'd wondered if she should assign some meaning to the fact he'd fallen asleep. Maybe it was a sign that she should step back and reevaluate her decision. After all, once she and Tony embarked on a physical relationship, there would be no turning back, at least for her. A line would be crossed. Everything that was between them would change. She mulled that through the night, which she'd spent in the bedroom she'd occupied these last several months. When the sun rose, however, she hadn't changed her mind. Gazing down at him now, she knew this was where she belonged. She wouldn't, couldn't, think beyond the here and now. She made fast work of the rest of the buttons and pushed the shirt back on his shoulders. When she reached for the waistband of his pants, he moved with lightning speed. Just that quick she found herself beneath him.

"If it is all right with you, I am done being patient and I am done letting you seduce me." He nipped at her jaw and started down.

"And if I say n-no?" Her breath caught as his fingers found and unfastened the front clasp of her bra.

Lowering his head, Tony said, "I will talk you into it."

CHAPTER ELEVEN

HEIDI scratched the cat behind one of his tattered ears as she sat on Rachel's couch in the studio apartment.

Rachel had moved in three weeks ago, and while she missed many of the luxuries in Tony's large house, including her proximity to Tony, it was good to have all of her belongings in one place—a place she owned.

Besides, she loved the space. The apartment was bright and airy. The commute to work couldn't be beat. And, now that everything was under one roof, she had access to everything she needed for her design work—day or night.

"So, which one?" she asked her sister, holding up two dresses.

"Go with the purple since you're trying to make a statement," Heidi said decisively, nodding to the dress on the hanger in Rachel's right hand.

The deep violet shift had black-lace-filled cutout bands on both of its sleeves, lending the otherwise basic garment an air of seduction. Rachel knew all about seduction these days. She'd been on both the giving and the receiving end with Tony. She hadn't made up her mind which she preferred. Power and surrender each held their own erotic allure.

"I think you're right."

"I know I'm right. I'm also jealous. Are you sure I can't

stow away in your luggage? Please! Please!" Heidi clasped her hands. "I don't want to stay here and look after your cat. I want to go to Rome."

Daphne had invited Rachel and Tony to a party at her home in Italy's capital city. Rachel was to be the guest of honor, even if it was her jewelry that would be the star attraction.

Daphne loved the piece Rachel had created for her. Given what she'd paid for the necklace, it was a good thing, too. Now, she was not satisfied to wait another year to introduce either the jewelry or the designer to her close friends. So she was insisting on hosting an intimate gathering. Tony already had warned Rachel that when it came to close friends, Daphne had a *few dozen* of them.

Her international career was as good as launched, Tony claimed since Daphne was already taking credit for having discovered Rachel. Even so, Rachel was nervous.

"I wish I could bring you. I wouldn't mind the moral support or the company."

"I'm guessing Tony would."

"It's not like that."

"Sure it is." But Heidi's words held no rancor. "Three's a crowd, especially at this point in a relationship."

"And what point might that be?"

Heidi grinned. "The I-can't-wait-to-get-you-naked-all-the-time point."

"Heidi."

"Seriously, Rach, you couldn't have snagged a better boyfriend. Tony's good-looking, successful, wealthy..." Her sister sighed. "And then there's that accent. Who can resist a man with an Italian accent?"

"Those aren't the reasons why I'm with him." Indeed it was more than that. But her sister misunderstood.

"He does make one heck of a rebound. I wonder if Mal

knows. Wouldn't it be great if he thought you'd been fooling around on him?"

Rachel was appalled and her tone reflected that. "I don't give a rat's behind about Mal and what he thinks, although I hope he knows I never broke my vows while we were married. And Tony is a lot more than a rebound. He's...He's..."

Heidi's eyes widened. "God, Rach. I'm sorry. I didn't mean anything I said."

She nodded.

"Does he know?" Heidi asked softly.

"Know what?"

"That you love him."

Rachel sank down on the couch next to her sister. "No. I didn't know myself until just now."

Oh, she'd had a sneaking suspicion, especially since their relationship had become intimate. But she'd dismissed it. Denied it. There was no denying it now.

"I love him," she said in a stunned whisper, her heart taking flight only to be brought up short by the tether of reality. When it came to women, Tony didn't do forever.

Heidi hugged her. "Is it okay if I'm happy for you?"

"How do you do this all the time?" Rachel asked as Tony fussed with the knot of his tie. They had arrived at his apartment in Rome the previous afternoon. She had yet to adapt to the time change. Indeed, she had yet to adapt to a lot of things, including her deepening feelings for Tony and where they might lead. She tried not to think about that, concentrating on the trip instead.

He misunderstood. Sending her a wink in the bureau mirror, he said, "You get used to wearing ties."

"I'm not talking about that. I'm talking about jetting back and forth across the Atlantic as often as you do.

I'm ready for bed—to sleep," she clarified when his eyebrows rose.

Despite the sternness of her tone, her body began to hum. This part of their relationship was easy. The man was insatiable, not that she was complaining. Especially since, for the first time in her life, the same could be said for her. She hadn't known herself to be such a sexual being. Nor had she ever imagined she possessed so many erogenous zones, with more being discovered, it seemed, every time they made love.

Unfortunately, even if Rachel hadn't been exhausted, she and Tony didn't have time even for a quick tussle between the sheets. They were expected at Daphne's within the hour, and Rachel was still wearing her robe and dithering about what to do with her hair.

"You get used to it. The key is to stay awake and not to sleep until it is nighttime where you are, rather than where you came from. Shall I make you some coffee or maybe another cup of espresso?"

She shook her head. "Thanks, but I'm feeling jittery enough about this evening without adding a jolt of caffeine."

Tony joined her on the settee tucked into the corner of his master suite. Draping an arm around her shoulders, he dropped a kiss on her temple.

"How many times must I tell you there is no need to be nervous? Daphne loves your designs. Her friends will, too, and not only because they know what a fan of yours Daphne has become."

Her introduction to Daphne's friends wasn't the sole source of her nerves. Tony moved in this world of wealth and privilege with great ease. He'd been a part of it for so long, it was second nature to him. But it was all new to Rachel, and she was mindful of the fact that while everything had turned out just fine for Cinderella in the end, the night of her big ball, she'd lost a shoe and dashed to her carriage just before it turned back into a pumpkin.

Rachel rested her head on Tony's shoulder. The scent of his cologne had her inhaling deeply. She felt his hand start to massage the space between her shoulder blades that always held the worst of her stress. His touch was comforting, thoughtful, sweet—until his other hand got involved and went from resting casually on her knee to stroking the inside of her thigh just above the hem of her robe.

"Tony."

"We have time," he whispered in her ear before nipping gently at the lobe.

"But—"

"We have time," he insisted again.

It wasn't his words as much as the position of his hand that convinced Rachel he was right.

DAPHNE'S apartment was not far from Tony's in one of Rome's most exclusive and pricey areas. Much like his, it offered unparalleled views of the city that, even in twilight, were spectacular. They arrived late, which Tony had assured her meant they were early. Half of the guests had yet to arrive.

"This is Italy. Punctuality is not our strong suit," he said with a rumbling laugh as he removed the silk wrap from around Rachel's shoulders.

Underneath, she was wearing the purple dress Heidi had suggested. Rachel had opted to wear only a pair of simple onyx drop earrings. She wanted Daphne's guests to try on her jewelry themselves, rather than see it on her. It would seem more exclusive that way.

"Rachel, welcome." Daphne kissed both of her cheeks

before doing the same to Tony. "It is good to see you both again."

"It is good to see you, too."

"Not everyone has arrived yet, but my friends who are here are dying to meet you, Rachel."

"I'm eager to meet them, as well."

Butterflies flitted around in Rachel's stomach as she said it. This was it, the official start of her new career. It was hard to fathom how far she had come in the months since her divorce—professionally as well as emotionally. She glanced at Tony. She couldn't have done it without him, on either account.

He smiled his encouragement as Daphne said, "Come, then. Let me introduce you."

It was all so surreal, Rachel thought as she followed Daphne through the penthouse apartment, taking in the twelve-foot ceilings and tall windows that were bracketed in rich silk panels that pooled on the floor. Rachel recognized many of the paintings that hung on the walls. They were done by some of the world's greatest artists, a few of them still living. She didn't have to ask if they were originals. This was Daphne Valero after all. She could afford the real thing and didn't bother with imitations. And she was wearing the necklace Rachel had designed for her. Surreal, indeed.

Daphne's guests were all women and included minor European royalty, a punk-rock star, an actress, the wives of two members of the Italian parliament, a prominent chef and an up-and-coming shoe designer from Milan whose career the perfume heiress had helped launch during fashion week the previous fall. All of them greeted Rachel not only as an equal but with a little awe. It was a heady feeling, to be sure.

"I am most intrigued by the amethyst bib necklace. You

must share with me your inspiration," an older woman named Greta pleaded. She looped one of her thin arms through Rachel's and led her to the center of the amply proportioned living room where Daphne had set up a table to display Rachel's work.

Display was an understatement. The table itself was a work of art, topped in a blanket of fragrant white rose petals. Thick pillar candles of varying heights flickered amid the black-velvet busts bearing Rachel's designs. Gemstones nestled in an assortment of precious metals, winking in the candlelight. Her breath caught at the sight.

"Congratulations, *carina*," Tony whispered from behind her. "I hope it is all right, but I requested the white roses on your behalf. As a designer, you have a right to determine how your work is displayed. That is something for you to consider in the future. Is it everything you dreamed?"

"More," she murmured, her eyes growing moist. "So much more."

The rest of the night was a blur. Champagne flowed. Black-vested waiters glided among the guests, carrying silver trays heavy with filled glasses and bite-size culinary masterpieces. Rachel sipped iced tea to keep from growing hoarse. She never stopped talking. The very people others were so in awe of, this evening were in awe of her. It was more than flattering. It was a huge boost to her confidence. She could handle the public facet of her new career.

"I must have this piece," Pia Costanzo said.

According to Tony, Pia was the wife of a high-ranking member of parliament and came from a family who owned a vineyard in Tuscany. She picked up an 18-carat-gold bubble cuff that was studded in rose-cut blue sapphires and diamonds. It retailed for more than fifty-thousand

American dollars. Not that any of the women at the party were worried about prices.

"That's a little tame for me," said the young woman next to her.

She was an actress known for her steamy roles on screen and her kinky bedroom exploits off. As such, she and Pia's paths normally would not have crossed. Pia's expression made it clear how she felt about being subjected to the woman's company now.

Daphne stepped in to head off a possible scene. "This one is more you, Tawny."

She selected a thick silver cuff studded in square-cut onyx stones and clasped it over the actress's tattooed wrist.

"I agree. And that ring." Tawny pointed to the silver dragonfly whose wings were imbedded with blue moonstones. "I must have that ring."

And so the evening went with Rachel's designs snapped up as if they were candy.

If there was one downside to the evening it was the way the women flitted about Tony, openly flirting with him, and leaving Rachel to wonder if there was a reason for their seeming familiarity. It was foolish to be jealous. He was with Rachel now. But the question, once raised in her mind, began to nag: How long would it last? How long before Tony Salerno grew bored with her and moved on? And could she handle being merely his business partner once he had?

It was closing in on two in the morning when they headed back to their hotel. Amazingly, at least from Rachel's perspective, they were not the last to leave.

"So how are you feeling?" Tony asked with a grin as a driver brought around their car. "Like you conquered the world perhaps?"

"More like the galaxy. Maybe even the universe."

"Then I hope you will be pleased when I tell you that Dona Lorenzo has invited us to Milan next week."

"The shoe designer that Daphne also discovered?" She was tall and raven-haired, with a dazzling smile that turned inappropriately carnal whenever her gaze had fallen on Tony during the evening, which had been often. Either something had gone on between them and ended, or the woman was hoping for something to start. Either way, it made Rachel uncomfortable.

"Yes. She has a photo shoot for a spread in one of my magazines, and would like to pair some of her shoes with some of your designs."

"You've said yes?"

"I told her I would need to ask you."

That made Rachel feel better. "Do you think we should go?"

"I think it is another good opportunity to ramp up the interest in your designs before taking on the American market. Create buzz, as they say." In the dim light of the car's interior, she saw him smile.

Buzz. That's what her head was doing right now. It was so crammed with ideas, images, impressions and questions, not all of which had to do with her career.

"Okay." She nodded. Then, unable to sit still any longer, she leaned forward and tapped the driver on the shoulder. "Can you stop here, please, er, *per favore*." To Tony, she said, "How do I say pull over?"

"Accostare qui," Tony told the driver. As the car was pulled to the curb, he asked Rachel, "What is wrong? Why are we stopping?"

"I want to…need to walk. It's not too far, is it?"

"A couple more blocks," he said. *"Carina?* Is everything all right?"

"Fine." But to Rachel's horror, her eyes filled with tears.

She tried to blink them back only to have a couple fat drops fall. Swiping at her damp cheeks, she said, "I'm sorry. I think the evening has caught up with me."

Tony took her hand, kissed the back of it before tucking it into the crook of his arm. "Let us walk, then."

The side streets were quiet at this time of night. The *click-click* of Rachel's heels the only sound until she heard the rushing of water. Around the next corner, the street opened up into a plaza with a fountain at its center.

"This is not Trevi," Tony said, referring to the mammoth masterpiece that featured Neptune on a horse-drawn seashell set against the walls of the Palazzo dei Duchi di Poli. "But it is said if you cast a coin in and make a wish it will come true."

Rachel sat on the low wall that surrounded the fountain. "All of my wishes have come true already."

"Have they? All of them?" He reached into his pocket and pulled out a couple of coins. "I worry that what I want most might need a little help."

He handed her one of the coins. Then, giving his a kiss for extra luck, he flipped it into the water. What had he wished, Rachel wondered? She knew better than to ask, not only because superstition dictated that wishes had to remain secret in order to come true. But because she was afraid of what his answer might be.

"Your turn."

She rubbed her thumb over the coin. She had the career she'd long dreamed of and she was with a man she had never dreamed would be interested in her. She'd told herself to be content with the here and now.

I wish for forever.

Just as Tony had, she kissed the coin before sending it flying.

CHAPTER TWELVE

RACHEL had never been on the set of a fashion shoot. Tony walked her through what he knew of them based on previous experience, explaining the importance of lighting and composition.

She nodded, nibbled her lower lip. Smiling to himself, he couldn't be sure if she'd heard a single word he'd said.

"I like the white rose petals," he remarked. They were scattered over the set and flowed out of a pair of snakeskin pumps. One of Rachel's rings was propped on the shoe's vamp.

"I requested them," she surprised him by saying. "I liked the way they looked on the display table at Daphne's."

"Taking my advice, I see."

"They are my designs, even if this isn't my shoot."

She'd come so far, in so short a time, he thought with no small measure of pride. "So, are white roses going to be your signature flower, something that connects one show and shoot to another? Beyond your jewelry, of course."

"Yes." She smiled. "Like a calling card. I have no intention of being difficult, but as you said, I am the designer. I need to have some control over the presentation."

"It is okay to be a little difficult, too." He lowered his voice. "I told Dona to be sure to have green tea on hand. I told her you require it."

"I require it?" Her eyes went wide before she blinked. "You make me sound like a diva."

He shrugged. "Your wants and needs are important. If you do not assert yourself, especially at this early stage, people such as Dona will decide things for you or take advantage. It was my way of leveling the playing field."

"With green tea."

"Yes." He was serious when he said, "You take a backseat to no one. If you do not like the way your designs are presented, you have only to say so. That is your prerogative and your right. Accept nothing short of perfection."

The shoot went well and wrapped up after only a few hours. Of course, other photographs had been taken the day before with models. Tony was retrieving Rachel's coat from the break area. When he turned around, he nearly ran over Dona.

"I wish the day didn't have to end so soon," she said in Italian. "I enjoy working with you, Tony."

"Rachel's designs paired well with your shoes," he said with a smile.

He tried to slip by her, but there was no way he could maneuver around her without brushing against her breasts. He knew exactly what she wanted. Dona had made it plain at Daphne's party in Rome, and all day long she had found reasons to touch him, going so far as to rest a hand on his thigh when they'd taken a break for lunch. She'd nibbled from the antipasto on his plate even. Rachel, who'd been seated across from him, had not looked happy. He couldn't blame her, but short of publicly humiliating Dona, he'd seen no way of ending the problem. He'd done his best to ignore her brazen behavior in the hope she would take a hint and cease.

Apparently, he had no such luck.

"Are you free tonight?" she asked.

"I am afraid not. Rachel and I are having dinner and taking in a show with some friends of mine."

"Perhaps tomorrow, then. You could stop by my studio when you are not babysitting your little friend."

She pressed a hand to his crotch and made a ribald suggestion that would have made a hedonist blush. Before he'd started seeing Rachel, Tony might have been tempted to find out if what Dona suggested was anatomically possible. Right now, he chuckled, but shook his head. "Sorry, but I will have to pass."

He caught a movement out of the corner of his eye. Rachel stood in the doorway, her lips pressed together, her gaze cool. Despite her limited grasp of Italian, Tony knew she had no need for an interpreter.

Far from being embarrassed, Dona said brazenly in English, "A rain check, then. I will look forward to hearing from you."

After giving him one last caress through his trousers, she retreated, pushing past Rachel with a smug smile on her face.

"Rach—" he began once they were alone.

"I'm all set to go if you are."

"About Dona—"

"Don't." She pinched her eyes closed for a moment and shook her head. "It doesn't matter."

"It does. The look on your face tells me as much." He reached for her arm, half expecting her to pull free. She didn't, but it was apparent she had already retreated from him in other ways. An unexpected ache throbbed in his chest. "You do not trust me. You think I am like the man you were married to. That I will be unfaithful."

"No. I don't believe that at all."

Her staunch denial did little to lessen his fears. "I did

nothing to encourage Dona's forward behavior today. Nothing. Just now, in here, she came on to me."

"I know that, Tony."

"You know. You know. You are not acting like you know." He scrubbed a hand over his face.

"How am I acting?" She crossed her arms over her chest.

He'd been involved with enough women that he knew a trap when he saw one. "I probably should have done more to discourage her. I just did not want to create a public scene."

"I know."

"Again with the *I know*," he shouted impatiently. "If you know, then what are we fighting about?"

"We aren't fighting. I know you won't cheat on me. You once told me that you are always faithful to a woman—for as long as you are with her."

The caveat at the end was what caught his attention. Tony frowned. Yes, he'd said that. He'd meant it at the time, too, because he'd been content with short-term romances that filled a physical need. He had much more than that with Rachel. He didn't want it to end. Not now. Not ever?

"I am happy with you. Rachel, I...I..."

A word he'd never said to a woman before hovered on the tip of his tongue. Love. *Santo cielo!* When had it happened? But then he knew. It hadn't occurred in one moment, but during a series of moments spread out over the course of several months. Attraction had come first, then friendship, a physical relationship and finally this deep, fulfilling and, at the moment, very frightening emotional tie.

Especially when he heard her say, "Yes, you are happy now, Tony."

"Do you think I am going somewhere? That there is someone else I wish to be with?"

"Right now, no. A month from now? A year? I don't know." The smile she gave him never reached her eyes. "It's not as if either of us has ever made any promises."

"Is that what you want, *carina*? Promises?"

Was that what *he* wanted? His palms were sweating. His stomach was in knots. He experienced no relief when she shook her head.

"No. I've had promises. I like what we have, too. We're happy together, now. That's more than enough."

"Yes."

That was exactly what he had always believed. So much so it had practically been his dating mantra. *Madonna mio.* He'd known he had changed. But it wasn't until this very moment that he realized how very much.

RACHEL spent another three days in Italy. It was all the time she could spare before she had to return home. The shop needed her, and she had deadlines to meet on pieces for her regular customers. Besides, Tony had work to do, as well. He had squeezed in an interview with a world-renowned chef during their trip to Milan for a piece he was doing on Mediterranean cooking. After Rachel returned to the States, he would be traveling down to Sicily for a week before heading over to Athens, Greece.

After the incident at the photo shoot, things between them had been somewhat strained. She tried not to let herself worry about losing him. She'd been foolish to think she could hold on to a man like Tony. Here in Italy, in his glitzy world among his glamorous circle, she'd realized just how different they were. Despite his deep love for his family, which brought him back to Michigan frequently, he was immersed in this lifestyle. And she was a novelty.

As Dona herself had told Rachel when she stopped by the hotel while Tony was out on his interview, "He will get bored with you soon enough. I do not mean this as an insult. It is just Tony's way." She'd laughed. "He will tire of me in time, too. But I should have been patient. I should have waited for him to finish with you before extending the invitation I did the other day. *Allora.* No hard feelings?"

Apparently, Dona's words were intended to serve as an apology. Some apology. Rachel hadn't bothered to tell Tony about the incident. She saw no point. But it served as a reminder to guard her heart. Mal's betrayal had hurt her. If she allowed it to, Tony's defection would destroy her.

"I have a surprise for you, *carina,*" Tony announced as he opened the car door for her.

Rachel was booked on a flight scheduled to leave Rome at nine o'clock that morning. By the same time tomorrow she would be in her cozy studio apartment in Rochester, fighting off jet lag and catching up on a couple of weeks' worth of business correspondence.

"What?"

"A little side trip."

"To where?"

"Venice."

Her eyes widened. "But my flight."

"I took the liberty of rescheduling for late tomorrow night. If that will not suit, I will change it back, but I thought it was a shame you did not get to see Venice. You said it was the one city in Italy you wanted to visit."

"You remember that?" It had been months ago. Long before they'd begun to date.

"I remember all sorts of things when it comes to you." He smiled. "So, Venice? It will be a whirlwind trip, but you can buy some Murano beads and go home inspired."

"I would like that."

Whirlwind wasn't the word for it. Tony had a friend who owned an estate on a small island in the Venice Lagoon. He was only too happy to loan Tony its use in return for a generous donation to a charity the man chaired. They took a helicopter from Rome to the island and his friend's boat from there to where the murky green waters flowed into the Grand Canal. She marveled at the Byzantine architecture of St. Mark's Basilica. They had a late lunch at a restaurant that overlooked the square before heading to a glass shop. Rachel watched the glass artists with interest, mesmerized by the beauty and fluidity of the glass before it hardened into the desired shape.

"Already I see your creative juices starting to flow," Tony remarked. "I predict you will be very busy upon your return home tomorrow."

He bought her a necklace of the famed beads, did the honors himself in putting it around her neck. He kissed her cheek afterward. Her heart thumped and then dropped into her stomach. Was this goodbye? Tony, after all, was well known for giving the women he left jewelry as a parting gift. He couldn't very well commission Rachel to make her own. Murano beads, then, would be the next best thing. She immediately chided herself for being ridiculous. But eventually…

"What are you thinking, *carina?*" He asked, lifting her chin so that she was forced to look him in the eye.

"I'm thinking about how much I am going to miss you," she said softly. It wasn't a lie.

Tony paced his Rome apartment. Rachel had been gone less than a week and already he was lonely and irritable and afraid. Yes, afraid. He was losing her.

Despite all of her reassurances, he could feel her pulling back, pulling away. It wasn't only the physical distance that bothered him, although for the first time in his life Rome no longer felt like home. No, it was the emotional distance that left him feeling anxious.

It was nothing that she'd said or done. Even after their fight that, according to her, wasn't a fight, they'd made love. And she'd seemed to enjoy their quick side trip to Venice. But the beads he'd given her had made her sad. She'd smiled, thanked him. Kissed him. But he knew her too well now. Something was wrong.

He'd tried to talk to her about it. He'd brought it up several times now, both while she was still in Italy and during phone calls to her in Michigan. She either sidestepped the issue or told him it was nothing.

Nothing. That was exactly what she expected from him. No future other than as business partners. Meanwhile, Tony had fallen in love. He couldn't lose her. He needed her in his life. But how to convince her of that? He'd always been a silver-tongued charmer. More than words, he needed a grand gesture, an over-the-top demonstration to prove to her beyond a shadow of a doubt that he meant what he planned to say.

Tony picked up the telephone and dialed without bothering to consider the time difference. He had an idea.

"Hello, Bill. This is a pleasant surprise." Rachel shook Tony's brother-in-law's hand and motioned for him to take a seat on one of the high stools at the glass counter. "Jenny tells me you are after something special."

"That's right. A ring. And of course I want you to design it."

"I'm happy to. How's Ava feeling?"

"Good. She says she's fat." He shook his head on a laugh. "She's claimed that the last two pregnancies, too. I think she looks beautiful."

Having seen Ava recently, Rachel had to agree. The two women had met for lunch. *Radiant* was the adjective that came to mind. Rachel chalked it up to overall happiness as much as pregnancy. She was a woman secure in her place in her man's heart.

"So you're here for a ring to make sure she knows how much you love her." Rachel smiled. "She's a lucky woman."

"I'm the one who fell in the gravy, but I don't mind letting her think that every now and again." He winked before folding his hands in front of him and growing serious. "So, how are things with you and Tony?"

"Oh, you know." She shrugged and scraped at the remnants of a price sticker on the counter with one of her thumb nails. "We've both been so busy."

"And then there's the long distance."

"Yes."

"It can't be easy, but then relationships rarely are. Especially ones that mean something. I talked to him the other day," Bill said. "He said he can't wait till he comes home again in six weeks. This time, I have a feeling he'll be around for a while longer."

She glanced up. "Why do you say that?"

He shrugged. "It's becoming harder for him to leave with so much waiting for him back here."

Bill was mistaken, she decided, but said politely, "I'm looking forward to seeing him."

She and Tony were in frequent contact, falling back into their usual routine of phone calls and emails. He no longer signed his missives Yours Patiently or simply Yours. These days, he signed them Yours Always. She tried not to attach much meaning to the change. Indeed, she was trying to be very careful about thinking beyond each call or note, except where it pertained to business.

She smiled at Bill, "About this ring, why don't you tell me what you have in mind?"

"I want the feature stone to be a diamond, two carats in a marquis cut. The stones you set around it can be your choice."

"You seem to know exactly what you want," she remarked.

He flushed. "It has to be perfect."

"I understand."

"It needs to make a statement. It needs to say, 'I love you. I can't live without you. I want to spend the rest of my life waking up next to you.'" He coughed. "Um, that's what the ring needs to say."

Oh, if only to hear Tony say all of that to her. She dabbed her eyes. "Sorry. I'm touched by the deep feelings you and Ava share."

Half of Bill's mouth curved up. "I remember how nervous I was when I asked her to marry me. I thought I would pass out before I managed to propose."

"That's sweet."

"It's hard, you know. Putting yourself on the line like that. They're just three little words, but saying 'I love you' is pretty scary when you mean it forever."

She thought it was an odd thing to say given how openly affectionate she knew Bill and Ava to be with one another.

"When do you need it?"

"The beginning of July." He rattled off the date. "That won't be a problem, will it?"

Rachel was desperately busy, but she meant it when she said, "For you, Bill, not at all. I'm a sucker for true love."

Tony called unexpectedly that night, rousing her from sleep just before midnight. She cradled the phone to her ear as she lay in bed, wishing he were next to her. But that wouldn't be the case for weeks.

"Is everything okay?" she asked.

"Everything is fine, except that I am missing you."

When he said things like that, it always caused her heart to flutter.

"Your brother-in-law came into the shop today."

"Did he?"

"He ordered a ring for Ava. It's going to be beautiful."

She told him a little about the design she had in mind.

"Nothing says I love you like a diamond," he remarked casually.

Beyond that Tony had little else to say on the subject, which surprised her since he usually peppered her with questions when it came to her designs. She chalked it up to the fact that it was for his sister. Maybe Tony felt awkward discussing such a personal ring. Or maybe it was what the ring represented. Her heart sank at that. As she knew only too well, Tony had never bought a ring for a woman. No rings. No diamonds. Only glittery trinkets that served to soften his goodbyes.

Their conversation ended not long after that. After hanging up, Rachel moved to the side of the bed where Tony usually slept. There was nothing she could do about the fact that she loved him, but she promised herself one thing. No matter what happened she wasn't going to regret their time together.

Six weeks passed in a blur, in part because Rachel was so busy. The first wave of advertising had begun, coinciding with the release of the photos from the fashion shoot in Italy. The glossy shots were featured in one of the most widely read fashion magazines. In those where Dona's shoes were paired with Rachel's jewelry, the gems stole the show, at least according to Tony. Rachel had to agree.

And even though it was petty of her, she hoped Dona thought so, too.

Now, seated in her shop, she stretched her back and yawned. The day had been a long one, but she was pleased with the finished product nestled in the Expressive Gems box on the counter. Bill's ring for Ava was ready. She almost hated to part with it. It was gorgeous and filled with such breathtaking sentiment.

It needs to say "I love you. I can't live without you. I want to spend the rest of my life waking up next to you."

Rachel smiled now, recalling Bill's words the day he'd placed the order. She was biased, but she believed she'd achieved his objective beautifully. Any woman would be proud to own such a ring.

She glanced at the clock. Even though the shop had officially closed for the day, Bill would be by any time to pick it up.

He had a special occasion in mind at which he would give the ring to Ava, he'd told Rachel. She envied the pair of them the night ahead.

She would be spending hers with Francis in the apartment. It would be her last alone for a few weeks, though. Or at least she was assuming that would be the case. Tony was coming in from Rome the following day.

She was pinching off the dying blooms from the floral arrangement when she heard a sharp knock at the door. Bill sounded impatient. She couldn't blame him. Smiling, she turned. Then she froze in place. It wasn't Bill who stood on the other side of the door. It was Tony, wearing his tuxedo and holding a bouquet of white roses.

Rachel tried to rein in her rioting emotions as she crossed to the door. Her fingers fumbled on the lock. On the other side of the door, Tony grinned.

"Wh-what are you doing here? When did you get back?"

The questions tumbled out in a flurry once she opened the door. His answer was to toss the roses aside and tug her into his arms for a kiss.

When it ended, he said, "I've been thinking about doing that all the way from the airport."

"I thought your flight wasn't due in until tomorrow." They'd made plans for dinner in the evening. A quiet one at his home. Just the two of them.

"I changed it." He shrugged. "I had somewhere very important I needed to be tonight."

Somewhere very important? Tony had never mentioned this very important date in any of their previous conversations. But here he was, dressed in formalwear. Meanwhile, she was in wrinkled linen and had replaced her stylish heels with flats out of deference to her aching arches.

"I don't want to keep you."

"I have time."

He tucked his hands into his pockets. She heard coins jingling. Why was he acting so evasive? Not only evasive, but, well, nervous. Dread shimmied up her spine. In a quiet voice she asked, "What are you doing here, Tony?"

He took a deep breath. Rachel caught hers.

"I came for the ring."

"The... Oh, the ring. You're here to pick it up for Bill."

She wanted to thump her forehead. Instead, she motioned to the counter near the back of the shop. "Let me just go and get it for you." Then he could leave and she could mentally regroup.

"First, may I have another kiss?"

For courage, it sounded like he added, but she must have heard him wrong. This time, his mouth lingered over hers. Something about this kiss was different, special. Or maybe that was all on her end.

I love you.

The words screamed through Rachel's head and very nearly made it past her lips. But she didn't say them. She couldn't be sure Tony would welcome such a complication in their relationship. Indeed, it might only succeed in making him end things sooner.

"What is this?" he asked after he drew away. He touched her cheeks. "Why are you crying?"

I love you. But again she held back, substituting "I've missed you" instead.

"I've missed you, too, *carina.* I..." He shook his head. "I need the ring."

"Right. The ring." She blinked away the rest of her tears and worked up a smile. "You said you had somewhere important to be, so I won't keep you."

He followed her to the counter. Instead of taking the ring and turning to leave, he sat down on one of the stools. "May I?" He tapped the lid of the box.

Work came to her rescue, as it had so many times in the past. "Of course. I wouldn't mind hearing what you think of it."

Tony opened the box and nodded his approval. "The diamond is perfect. Just the right size. What made you go with the mixed sapphires around it?"

"All the colors, they reminded me of the Murano beads I brought back from Venice."

"They are festive."

"Yes, happy." She thought of the years of tradition that went into creating them. "Enduring."

"That is what a good marriage should be like, or so I understand."

Rachel couldn't speak from experience, but she agreed. "Do you think your sister will like it?"

"Oh, Ava would love this." He took the ring from its

perch in the box. The diamond caught the light. "But it is not for her."

Rachel frowned. "But Bill said he wanted me to make her a ring. He—"

"Lied." Tony's gaze was on her. "I asked him to. The ring, it is for me, Rachel."

"But why?"

The corners of his mouth curved. This wasn't his bedroom smile. And that look in his eyes, it was one she had never seen before. "Do you really not know, *carina?*"

"Bill said the ring needed to say I love you." Her gaze connected with Tony as she said it aloud.

"Yes. That is what the ring needed to say. I needed it to speak for me, Rachel. So you would believe me."

"You lo—" She shook her head. "I want to hear you say it. I *need* to hear you, Tony."

Tony always came across as so self-assured. But his guard was down now. She saw vulnerability. She saw the emotion there even before he gave it voice.

"I love you, Rachel. I have fallen in love with you in a million small ways over these last several months."

Fresh tears spilled onto her cheeks. "I love you, too."

She watched his eyes pinch shut a moment, almost as if he hadn't been sure of her feelings.

"Being away from you, it has been torture. I know our careers will keep us busy, but I am hoping that wherever we have to travel, we will be together."

"What exactly are you saying?" she whispered, even though she thought she knew.

He pulled the ring from the box, took her left hand. She expected him to slip it on her finger.

He got down on one knee first, a jet-setting playboy eager to trade in his bachelor status.

"Will you marry me, Rachel? Will you be my wife and partner in all things?"

She was laughing when she said yes, crying as he pushed the ring over her knuckle.

"What do you know?" he murmured, straightening and pulling her into his arms. "The fit is perfect."

Smiling up at her husband-to-be, Rachel wholeheartedly agreed.

EPILOGUE

NEARLY every pew at Saint Cecilia Catholic Church was filled. The guests shifted in their seats, turning toward the back as the music started. The doors opened. Rachel was there. Smiling. A vision in white lace.

Tony stood at the altar, Bill at his side.

"I recommend you start breathing," his brother-in-law whispered. "You'll pass out otherwise."

Tony did feel light-headed. And happy. Ridiculously so, as his gaze connected with Rachel's. She was his bride. His future. She was on her father's arm and Griff was beaming. He might have come late to fatherhood, but he had been taking his role seriously this past year. So seriously that he'd taken Tony out for a drink the week before and then given him a lecture.

"If you break my daughter's heart, I'll break you." The look on the older man's face had made it clear that he meant it.

It was the look on Rachel's face now that held Tony's attention.

"Who gives this woman?" the priest asked when she reached the altar.

"Her mother and I," Griff said.

He placed her hand in Tony's. "Remember what I said," Griff whispered before withdrawing.

Tony smiled. With Rachel's hand tucked in his, he turned to the priest. Their life together was about to start.

* * * * *

REQUEST YOUR FREE BOOKS!
2 FREE NOVELS PLUS 2 FREE GIFTS!

Harlequin®

Romance

From the Heart, For the Heart

YES! Please send me 2 FREE Harlequin® Romance novels and my 2 FREE gifts (gifts are worth about $10). After receiving them, if I don't wish to receive any more books, I can return the shipping statement marked "cancel". If I don't cancel, I will receive 6 brand-new novels every month and be billed just $4.09 per book in the U.S. or $4.49 per book in Canada. That's a savings of at least 14% off the cover price! It's quite a bargain! Shipping and handling is just 50¢ per book in the U.S. and 75¢ per book in Canada.* I understand that accepting the 2 free books and gifts places me under no obligation to buy anything. I can always return a shipment and cancel at any time. Even if I never buy another book, the two free books and gifts are mine to keep forever.

116/316 HDN FESE

Name _____ (PLEASE PRINT) _____

Address _____ Apt. #

City _____ State/Prov. _____ Zip/Postal Code

Signature (if under 18, a parent or guardian must sign) _____

Mail to the **Reader Service:**
IN U.S.A.: P.O. Box 1867, Buffalo, NY 14240-1867
IN CANADA: P.O. Box 609, Fort Erie, Ontario L2A 5X3

Not valid for current subscribers to Harlequin Romance books.

**Are you a subscriber to Harlequin Romance books
and want to receive the larger-print edition?
Call 1-800-873-8635 or visit www.ReaderService.com.**

* Terms and prices subject to change without notice. Prices do not include applicable taxes. Sales tax applicable in N.Y. Canadian residents will be charged applicable taxes. Offer not valid in Quebec. This offer is limited to one order per household. All orders subject to credit approval. Credit or debit balances in a customer's account(s) may be offset by any other outstanding balance owed by or to the customer. Please allow 4 to 6 weeks for delivery. Offer available while quantities last.

Your Privacy—The Reader Service is committed to protecting your privacy. Our Privacy Policy is available online at www.ReaderService.com or upon request from the Reader Service.

We make a portion of our mailing list available to reputable third parties that offer products we believe may interest you. If you prefer that we not exchange your name with third parties, or if you wish to clarify or modify your communication preferences, please visit us at www.ReaderService.com/consumerschoice or write to us at Reader Service Preference Service, P.O. Box 9062, Buffalo, NY 14269. Include your complete name and address.

HR11B

HARLEQUIN Romance

At their grandmother's request, three estranged
sisters return home for Christmas to the small town
of Beckett's Run. Little do they know that this family
reunion will reveal long-buried secrets...
and new-found love.

Discover the magic of Christmas in a brand-new
Harlequin® Romance miniseries.

In October 2012, find yourself
SNOWBOUND IN THE EARL'S CASTLE
by **Fiona Harper**

Be enchanted in November 2012 by a
SLEIGH RIDE WITH THE RANCHER
by **Donna Alward**

And be mesmerized in December 2012 by
MISTLETOE KISSES WITH THE BILLIONAIRE
by **Shirley Jump**

Available wherever books are sold.

*Sensational author Kate Hewitt brings you
a sneak-peek excerpt from THE DARKEST OF SECRETS,
the intensely powerful first story
in her new Harlequin® Presents® miniseries,*
THE POWER OF REDEMPTION.

* * *

"You're attracted to me, Grace."

"It doesn't matter."

"Do you still not trust me?" he asked quietly. "Is that it? Are you afraid—of me?"

"I'm not afraid of you," she said, and meant it. She might not trust him, but she didn't fear him. She simply didn't want to let him have the kind of power opening your body or heart to someone would give. And then of course there were so many reasons not to get involved.

"What, then?" She just shook her head. "I know you've been hurt," he said quietly and she let out a sad little laugh. He was painting his own picture of her, she knew then, a happy little painting like one a child might make. Too bad he had the wrong paint box.

"And how do you know that?" she asked.

"It's evident in everything you do and say—"

"No, it isn't." She *had* been hurt, but not the way he thought. She'd never been an innocent victim, as much as she wished things could be that simple. And she knew, to her own shame and weakness, that she wouldn't say anything. She didn't want him to look at her differently. With judgment rather than compassion, scorn instead of sympathy.

"Why can't you get involved, then, Grace?" Khalis asked. "It was just a kiss, after all." He'd moved to block the doorway, even though Grace hadn't yet attempted to leave. His face looked harsh now, all hard angles and narrowed eyes, even though his body remained relaxed. A man of contradictions—or was it simply deception? Which was the real man, Grace wondered, the smiling man who'd rubbed her feet so gently, or the angry son who refused to grieve for the family he'd just lost? Or was he both, showing one face to the world and hiding another, just as she was?

Khalis Tannous has ruthlessly eradicated every hint of corruption and scandal from his life. But the shadows haunting the eyes of his most recent—most beautiful— employee aren't enough to dampen his desire. Grace can foresee the cost of giving in to temptation, but will she risk everything she has for a night in his bed?

Find out on September 18, 2012, wherever books are sold!

celebrating
15 YEARS

Love Inspired

Another heartwarming installment of

← **TEXAS TWINS** →

Two sets of twins, torn apart by family secrets,
find their way home

When big-city cop Grayson Wallace visits an elementary
school for career day, he finds his heartstrings
unexpectedly tugged by a six-year-old fatherless boy and
his widowed mother, Elise Lopez. Now he can't get the
struggling Lopezes off his mind. All he can think about
is what family means—especially after discovering
the identical twin brother he hadn't known he had
in Grasslands. Maybe a trip to ranch country is just
what he, Elise and little Cory need.

Look-Alike Lawman
by Glynna Kaye

*Available October 2012
wherever books are sold.*

www.LoveInspiredBooks.com

LI87770

Sometimes love strikes in the most unexpected circumstances...

Soon-to-be single mom Antonia Wright isn't looking for romance, especially from a cowboy. But when rancher and single father Clayton Traub rents a room at Antonia's boardinghouse, Wright's Way, she isn't prepared for the attraction that instantly sizzles between them or the pain she sees in his big brown eyes. Can Clay and Antonia trust their hearts and build the family they've always dreamed of?

Don't miss

THE MAVERICK'S READY-MADE FAMILY

by Brenda Harlen

Available this October from Harlequin® Special Edition®

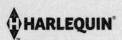

HARLEQUIN®

n o c t u r n e™

Satisfy your paranormal cravings with two dark
and sensual new werewolf tales from
Harlequin® Nocturne™!

FOREVER WEREWOLF
by Michele Hauf

Can sexy, charismatic werewolf Trystan Hawkes win the
heart of Alpine pack princess Lexi Connors—or will dark
family secrets cost him the pack's trust…and her love?

THE WOLF PRINCESS
by Karen Whiddon

Will Dr. Braden Streib risk his life to save royal wolf shifter
Princess Alisa—even if it binds them inescapably together
in a battle against a deadly faction?

**Plus look for a reader-favorite story
included in each book!**

2 GREAT
NOVELS
SAME GREAT
PRICE

Available September 18, 2012